THE MAN WHO JAPED

BOOKS BY PHILIP K. DICK

The Exegesis of Philip K. Dick

PHILIP K. DICK

‡

THE MAN WHO JAPED

‡

MARINER BOOKS
HOUGHTON MIFFLIN HARCOURT
Boston   New York

First Mariner Books edition 2012

www.hmhbooks.com

Library of Congress Cataloging-in-Publication Data is available.

ISBN 978-0-547-57253-6

Book design by Melissa Lotfy

Printed in the United States of America

DOC 10 9 8 7 6 5 4 3 2 1

Originally published in the United States by
Ace Books, Inc., New York, in 1956.

THE MAN WHO JAPED

1

At seven a.m., Allen Purcell, the forward-looking young president of the newest and most creative of the Research Agencies, lost a bedroom. But he gained a kitchen. The process was automatic, controlled by an iron-oxide-impregnated tape sealed in the wall. Allen had no authority over it, but the transfiguration was agreeable to him; he was already awake and ready to rise.

Squinting and yawning and now on his feet, he fumbled for the manual knob that released the stove. As usual the stove was stuck half in the wall and half out into the room. But all that was needed was a firm push. Allen pushed, and, with a wheeze, the stove emerged.

He was king of his domain: this one-room apartment within sight of the — blessed — Morec spire. The apartment was hard won. It had been his heritage, deeded to him by his family; the lease had been defended for over forty years. Its thin plasterboard walls formed a box of priceless worth; it was an empty space valued beyond money.

The stove, properly unfolded, became also sink and table and food cupboard. Two chairs hinged out from its underside, and beneath the stored supplies were dishes. Most of the room was consumed, but sufficient space remained in which to dress.

His wife Janet, with difficulty, had gotten into her slip. Now, frowning, she held an armload of skirt and looked around her in bewilderment. The central heating had not penetrated to their apartment as yet, and Janet shivered. In the cold autumn mornings she awoke with fright; she had been his wife three years but she had never adjusted to the shifts of the room.

"What's the matter?" he asked, shedding his pajamas. The air, to him, was invigorating; he took a deep breath.

"I'm going to reset the tape. Maybe for eleven." She resumed dressing, a slow process with much wasted motion.

"The oven door," he said, opening the oven for her. "Lay your things there, like always."

Nodding, she did so. The Agency had to be opened promptly at eight, which meant getting up early enough to make the half-hour walk along the clogged lanes. Even now sounds of activity filtered up from the ground level, and from other apartments. In the hall, scuffling footsteps were audible; the line was forming at the community bathroom.

"You go ahead," he said to Janet, wanting her dressed and ready for the day. As she started off, he added: "Don't forget your towel."

Obediently, she collected her satchel of cosmetics, her soap and toothbrush and towel and personal articles, and left. Neighbors assembled in the hall greeted her.

"Morning, Mrs. Purcell."

Janet's sleepy voice: "Morning, Mrs. O'Neill." And then the door closed.

When his wife was gone, Allen shook two corto-thiamin capsules from the medicine well. Janet owned all sorts of pills and sprays; in her early teens she had picked up undulant fever, one of the plagues revived by the attempt to create natural farms on the colony planets. The corto-thiamin was for his hangover.

Last night he had drunk three glasses of wine, and on an empty stomach.

Entering the Hokkaido area had been a calculated risk. He had worked late at the Agency, until ten o'clock. Tired, but still restless, he had locked up and then rolled out a small Agency ship, a one-man sliver used to deliver rush orders to T-M. In the ship he had scooted out of Newer York, flown aimlessly, and finally turned East to visit Gates and Sugermann. But he hadn't stayed long; by eleven he was on his way back. And it had been necessary. Research was involved.

His Agency was totally outclassed by the giant four that made up the industry. Allen Purcell, Inc. had no financial latitude and no backlog of ideas. Its packets were put together from day to day. His staff—artists, historian, moral consultant, dictionist, dramatist—tried to anticipate future trends rather than working from patterns that had been successful in the past. This was an advantage, as well as a defect. The big four were hidebound; they constructed a standard packet perfected over the years, basically the time-tested formula used by Major Streiter himself in the days before the revolution. Moral Reclamation, in those days, had consisted of wandering troups of actors and lecturers delivering messages, and the major had been a genius at media. The basic formula was, of course, adequate, but new blood was needed. The major himself had been new blood; originally a powerful figure in the Afrikaans Empire—the re-created Transvaal State—he had revitalized the moral forces lying dormant in his own age.

"Your turn," Janet said, returning. "I left the soap and towel, so go right in." As he started from the room she bent to get out the breakfast dishes.

Breakfast took the usual eleven minutes. Allen ate with customary directness; the corto-thiamin had eliminated his queasiness. Across from him Janet pushed her half-finished food away and began combing her hair. The window — with a touch of the switch — doubled as a mirror: another of the ingenious space-savers developed by the Committee's Housing Authority.

"You didn't get in until late," Janet said presently. "Last night, I mean." She glanced up. "Did you?"

Her question surprised him, because he had never known her to probe. Lost in the haze of her own uncertainties, Janet was incapable of venom. But, he realized, she was not probing. She was apprehensive. Probably she had lain awake wondering if he were all right, lain with her eyes open staring at the ceiling until eleven-forty, at which time he had made his appearance. As he had undressed, she had said nothing; she had kissed him as he slid in beside her, and then she had gone to sleep.

"Did you go to Hokkaido?" she wondered.

"For a while. Sugermann gives me ideas . . . I find his talk stimulating. Remember the packet we did on Goethe? The business about lens-grinding? I never heard of that until Sugermann mentioned it. The optics angle made a good Morec — Goethe saw his real job. Prisms before poetry."

"But —" She gestured, a familiar nervous motion of her hands. "Sugermann's an egghead."

"Nobody saw me." He was reasonably certain of that; by ten o'clock Sunday night most people were in bed. Three glasses of wine with Sugermann, a half hour listening to Tom Gates play Chicago jazz on the phonograph, and that was all. He had done it a number of times before, and without untoward difficulty.

Bending down, he picked up the pair of oxfords he had worn. They were mud-spattered. And, across each, were great drops of dried red paint.

"That's from the art department," Janet said. She had, in the first year of the Agency, acted as his receptionist and file clerk, and she knew the office layout. "What were you doing with red paint?"

He didn't answer. He was still examining the shoes.

"And the mud," Janet said. "And look." Reaching down, she plucked a bit of grass dried to the sole of one shoe. "Where did you find grass at Hokkaido? Nothing grows in those ruins . . . it's contaminated, isn't it?"

"Yes," he admitted. It certainly was. The island had been saturated during the war, bombed and bathed and doctored and infested with every possible kind of toxic and lethal substance. Moral Reclamation was useless, let alone gross physical rebuilding. Hokkaido was as sterile and dead as it had been in 1972, the final year of the war.

"It's domestic grass," Janet said, feeling it. "I can tell." She had lived most of her life on colony planets. "The texture's smooth. It wasn't imported . . . it grows here on Earth."

With irritation he asked: "Where on Earth?"

"The Park," Janet said. "That's the only place grass grows. The rest is all apartments and offices. You must have been there last night."

Outside the window of the apartment the — blessed — Morec spire gleamed in the morning sun. Below it was the Park. The Park and spire comprised the hub of Morec, its *omphalos*. There, among the lawns and flowers and bushes, was the statue of Major Streiter. It was the official statue, cast during his lifetime. The statue had been there one hundred and twenty-four years.

"I walked through the Park," he admitted. He had stopped eating; his "eggs" were cooling on his plate.

"But the paint," Janet said. In her voice was the vague, troubled fear with which she met every crisis, the helpless sense of foreboding that always seemed to paralyze her ability to act.

"You didn't do anything wrong, did you?" She was, obviously, thinking of the lease.

Rubbing his forehead, Allen got to his feet. "It's seven-thirty. I'll have to start to work."

Janet also rose. "But you didn't finish eating." He always finished eating. "You're not sick, are you?"

"Me," he said. "Sick?" He laughed, kissed her on the mouth, and then found his coat. "When was I last sick?"

"Never," she murmured, troubled and watching him. "There's never anything the matter with you."

At the base of the housing unit, businessmen were clustered at the block warden's table. The routine check was in progress, and Allen joined the group. The morning smelled of ozone, and its clean scent helped clear his head. And it restored his fundamental optimism.

The Parent Citizens Committee maintained a female functionary for each housing unit, and Mrs. Birmingham was typical: plump, florid, in her middle fifties, she wore a flowered and ornate dress and wrote out her reports with a powerfully authoritative fountain pen. It was a respected position, and Mrs. Birmingham had held the post for years.

"Good morning, Mr. Purcell." She beamed as his turn arrived.

"Hello, Mrs. Birmingham." He tipped his hat, since block wardens set great store by the little civilities. "Looks like a nice day, assuming it doesn't cloud up."

"Rain for the crops," Mrs. Birmingham said, which was a joke. Virtually all foods and manufactured items were brought in by autofac rocket; the limited domestic supply served only as a standard of judgment, a kind of recalled ideal. The woman made a note on her long yellow pad. "I . . . haven't seen your lovely wife yet, today."

Allen always alibied for his wife's tardiness. "Janet's getting ready for the Book Club meeting. Special day: she's been promoted to treasurer."

"I'm so glad," Mrs. Birmingham said. "She's such a sweet girl. A bit shy, though. She should mix more with people."

"That's certainly true," he agreed. "She was brought up in the wide open spaces. Betelgeuse 4. Rocks and goats."

He had expected that to end the interview — his own conduct was rarely in question — but suddenly Mrs. Birmingham became rigid and business-like. "You were out late last night, Mr. Purcell. Did you have a good time?"

Lord, he cursed. A juvenile must have spotted him. "Not very." He wondered how much it had seen. If it tagged him early in the trip it might have followed the whole way.

"You visited Hokkaido," Mrs. Birmingham stated.

"Research," he said, assuming the posture of defense. "For the Agency." This was the great dialectic of the moral society, and, in a perverse way, he enjoyed it. He was facing a bureaucrat who operated by rote, whereas *he* struck through the layers of habit and hit directly. This was the success of his Agency, and it was the success of his personal life. "Telemedia's needs take precedence over personal feeling, Mrs. Birmingham. You certainly understand that."

His confidence did the trick, and Mrs. Birmingham's saccharine smile returned. Making a scratch with her pen she asked: "Will we see you at the block meeting next Wednesday? That's just the day after tomorrow."

"Certainly," Allen said. Over the decades he had learned to endure the interminable interchange, the stuffy presence of his neighbors packed together in one room. And the whirr of the juveniles as they surrendered their tapes to the Committee representatives. "But I'm afraid I won't have much to contribute." He was too busy with his ideas and plans to care who lapsed and in what way. "I've been up to my neck in work."

"Perhaps," Mrs. Birmingham said, in a partly bantering, partly haughty thought-for-this-week voice, "there might be a few criticisms of *you*."

"Of me?" He winced with shock, and felt ill.

"It seems to me that when I was glancing over the reports, I noticed your name. Perhaps not. I could be mistaken. Goodness." She laughed lightly. "If so it's certainly the first time in years. But none of us is perfect; we're all mortal."

"Hokkaido?" he demanded. *Or afterward.* The paint, the grass. There it was in a rush: the wet grass sparkling and slithering under him as he coasted dizzily downhill. The swaying staffs of trees. Above, as he lay gaping on his back, the dark-swept sky; clouds were figments of matter against the blackness. And he, lying stretched out, arms out, swallowing stars.

"Or afterward?" he demanded, but Mrs. Birmingham had turned to the next man in line.

2

THE LOBBY OF the Mogentlock Building was active and stirring with noise, a constant coming-and-going of busy people as Allen approached the elevator. Because of Mrs. Birmingham he was late. The elevator politely waited.

"Good morning, Mr. Purcell." The elevator's taped voice greeted him, and then the doors shut. "Second floor Bevis and Company Import-Export. Third floor American Music Federation. Fourth floor Allen Purcell, Inc. Research Agency." The elevator halted and opened its door.

In the outer reception lounge, Fred Luddy, his assistant, wandered about in a tantrum of discomfort.

"Morning," Allen murmured vaguely, taking off his coat.

"Allen, *she's here.*" Luddy's face flushed scarlet. "She got here before I did; I came up and there she was, sitting."

"Who? Janet?" He had a mental image of a Committee representative driving her from the apartment and canceling the lease. Mrs. Birmingham, with smiles, closing in on Janet as she sat absently combing her hair.

"Not Mrs. Purcell," Luddy said. He lowered his voice to a rasp. "It's Sue Frost."

Allen involuntarily craned his neck, but the inner door was

closed. If Sue Frost was really sitting in there, it marked the first time a Committee Secretary had paid a call on him.

"I'll be darned," he said.

Luddy yelped. "She wants to see you!"

The Committee functioned through a series of departmental secretaries directly responsible to Ida Pease Hoyt, the linear descendant of Major Streiter. Sue Frost was the administrator of Telemedia, which was the official government trust controlling mass communications. He had never dealt with Mrs. Frost, or even met her; he worked with the acting Director of T-M, a weary-voiced, bald-headed individual named Myron Mavis. It was Mavis who bought packets.

"What's she want?" Allen asked. Presumably, she had learned that Mavis was taking the Agency's output, and that the Agency was relatively new. With a sinking dread he anticipated one of the Committee's gloomy, protracted investigations. "Better have Doris block my incoming calls." Doris was one of his secretaries. "You take over until Mrs. Frost and I are through talking."

Luddy followed after him in a dance of prayer. "Good luck, Allen. I'll hold the fort for you. If you want the books —"

"Yes, I'll call you." He opened the office door, and there was Sue Frost.

She was tall, and she was rather large-boned and muscular. Her suit was a simple hard weave, dark gray in color. She wore a flower in her hair, and she was altogether a strikingly handsome woman. At a guess, she was in her middle fifties. There was little or no softness to her, nothing of the fleshy and over-dressed motherliness that he saw in so many Committee women. Her legs were long, and, as she rose to her feet, her right hand lifted to welcome him in a forthright — almost masculine — handshake.

"Hello, Mr. Purcell," she said. Her voice was not overly expressive. "I hope you don't mind my showing up this way, unannounced."

"Not at all," he murmured. "Please sit down."

She reseated herself, crossed her legs, contemplated him. Her eyes, he noticed, were an almost colorless straw. A strong kind of substance, and highly polished.

"Cigarette?" He extended his case, and she accepted a cigarette with a nod of thanks. He took one also, feeling like a gauche young man in the company of an older and more experienced woman.

He couldn't help thinking that Sue Frost was the type of urbane career woman ultimately not proposed to by the hero of Blake-Moffet's packets. There was an unsympathetic firmness about her. She was decidedly not the girl from next door.

"Undoubtedly," Sue Frost began, "you recognize this." She unraveled the winding of a manila folder and displayed a sheaf of script. On the cover of the sheaf was his Agency's stamp; she had one of his packets, and she evidently had been reading it.

"Yes," he admitted. "That's one of ours."

Sue Frost leafed through the packet, then laid it down on Allen's desk. "Myron accepted this last month. Then he had qualms and he sent it along the line to me. I had a chance to go over it this weekend."

Now the packet was turned so that Allen could catch the title. It was a high-quality piece he had personally participated in; as it stood it could have gone over any of T-M's media.

"Qualms," Allen said. "How do you mean?" He had a deep, cold sensation, as if he were involved in some eerie religious ritual. "If the packet won't go, then turn it back to us. We'll create a credit; we've done it before."

"The packet is beautifully handled," Mrs. Frost said, smoking. "No, Myron certainly didn't want it back. Your theme concerns this man's attempt to grow an apple tree on a colony planet. But the tree dies. The Morec of it is —" She again picked up the packet. "I'm not certain what the Morec is. Shouldn't he have tried to grow it?"

"Not there," Allen said.

"You mean it belonged on Earth?"

"I mean he should have been working for the good of society, not off somewhere nourishing a private enterprise. He saw the colony as an end in itself. But they're means. *This* is the center."

"*Omphalos,*" she agreed. "The navel of the universe. And the tree —"

"The tree symbolizes an Earth product that withers when it's transplanted. His spiritual side died."

"But he couldn't have grown it here. There's no room. It's all city."

"Symbolically," he explained. "He should have put down his roots here."

Sue Frost was silent for a moment, and he sat smoking uneasily, crossing and uncrossing his legs, feeling his tension grow, not diminish. Nearby, in another office, the switchboard buzzed. Doris' typewriter clacked.

"You see," Sue Frost said, "this conflicts with a fundamental. The Committee has put billions of dollars and years of work into outplanet agriculture. We've done everything possible to seed domestic plants in the colonies. They're supposed to supply us with our food. People realize it's a heartbreaking task, with endless disappointments . . . and you're saying that the outplanet orchards will fail."

Allen started to speak and then changed his mind. He felt absolutely defeated. Mrs. Frost was gazing at him searchingly, expecting him to defend himself in the usual fashion.

"Here's a note," she said. "You can read it. Myron's note on this, when it came to me."

The note was in pencil and went:

"Sue —

    The same outfit again. Top-drawer, but too coy. You decide.

M."

"What's he mean?" Allen said, now angered.

"He means the Morec doesn't come across." She leaned toward him. "Your Agency has been in this only three years. You started out very well. What do you currently gross?"

"I'd have to see the books." He got to his feet. "May I get Luddy in here? I'd like him to see Myron's note."

"Certainly," Mrs. Frost said.

Fred Luddy entered the office stiff-legged with apprehension. "Thanks," he muttered, as Allen gave him the packet. He read the note, but his eyes showed no spark of consciousness. He seemed tuned to invisible vibrations; the meaning reached him through the tension of the air, rather than the pencilled words.

"Well," he said finally, in a daze. "You can't win them all."

"We'll take this packet back, naturally." Allen began to strip the note from it, but Mrs. Frost said:

"Is that your only response? I told you we want it; I made that clear. But we can't take it in the shape it's in. I think you should know that it was my decision to give your Agency the go-ahead. There was some dispute, and I was brought in from the first." From the manila folder she took a second packet, a familiar one. "Remember this? May, 2112. We argued for hours. Myron liked this, and I liked it. Nobody else did. Now Myron has cold feet." She tossed the packet, the first the Agency had ever done, onto the desk.

After an interval Allen said: "Myron's getting tired."

"Very." She nodded agreeably.

Hunched over, Fred Luddy said: "Maybe we've been going at it too fast." He cleared his throat, cracked his knuckles and glanced at the ceiling. Drops of warm sweat sparkled in his hair and along his smoothly-shaved jowls. "We kind of got — excited."

Speaking to Mrs. Frost, Allen said: "My position is simple. In that packet, we made the Morec that Earth is the center. That's the real fundamental, and I believe it. If I didn't believe it I couldn't have developed the packet. I'll withdraw the packet but I won't change it. I'm not going to preach morality without practicing it."

Quakily, in a spasm of agonized back-pedalling, Luddy muttered: "It's not a moral question, Al. It's a question of clarity. The Morec of that packet doesn't come across." His voice had a ragged, guilty edge; Luddy knew what he was doing and he was ashamed. "I — see Mrs. Frost's point. Yes I do. It looks as if we're scuttling the agricultural program, and naturally we don't mean that. Isn't that so, Al?"

"You're fired," Allen said.

They both stared at him. Neither of them grasped that he was serious, that he had really done it.

"Go tell Doris to make out your check." Allen took the packet from the desk and held onto it. "I'm sorry, Mrs. Frost, but I'm the only person qualified to speak for the Agency. We'll credit you for this packet and submit another. All right?"

She stubbed out her cigarette, rising, at the same time, to her feet. "It's your decision."

"Thanks," he said, and felt a release of tension. Mrs. Frost understood his stand, and approved. And that was crucial.

"I'm sorry," Luddy muttered, ashen. "That was a mistake on my part. The packet is fine. Perfectly sound as it now exists." Plucking at Allen's sleeve, he drew him off in the corner. "I admit I made a mistake." His voice sank to a jumpy whisper. "Let's discuss this further. I was simply trying to develop one possible viewpoint among many. You want me to express myself; I mean, it seems senseless to penalize me for working in the best interests of the Agency, as I see it."

"I meant what I said," Allen said.

"You did?" Luddy laughed. "Naturally you meant it. You're the boss." He was shaking. "You really weren't kidding?"

Collecting her coat, Mrs. Frost moved toward the door. "I'd like to look over your Agency while I'm here. Do you mind?"

"Not at all," Allen said. "I'd be glad to show it to you. I'm quite proud of it." He opened the door for her, and the two of them walked out into the hall. Luddy remained in the office, a sick, erratic look on his face.

"I don't care for him," Mrs. Frost said. "I think you're better off without him."

"That wasn't any fun," Allen said. But he was feeling better.

3

IN THE HALL outside Myron Mavis' office, the Telemedia workers were winding up their day. The T-M building formed a connected hollow square. The open area in the center was used for outdoor sets. Nothing was in process now, because it was five-thirty and everybody was leaving.

From a pay phone, Allen Purcell called his wife. "I'll be late for dinner," he said.

"Are — you all right?"

"I'm fine," he said. "But you go ahead and eat. Big doings, big crisis at the Agency. I'll catch something down here." He added, "I'm at Telemedia."

"For very long?" Janet asked anxiously.

"Maybe for a long, long time," he said, and hung up.

As he rejoined Sue Frost, she said to him, "How long did Luddy work for you?"

"Since I opened the Agency." The realization was sobering: three years. Presently he added: "That's the only person I've ever let go."

At the back of the office, Myron Mavis was turning over duplicates of the day's output to a bonded messenger of the Committee. The duplicates would be put on permanent file; in case of an investigation the material was there to examine.

To the formal young messenger, Mrs. Frost said: "Don't leave. I'm going back; you can go with me."

The young man retired discreetly with his armload of metal drums. His uniform was the drab khaki of the Cohorts of Major Streiter, a select body composed of male descendants of the founder of Morec.

"A cousin," Mrs. Frost said. "A very distant cousin-in-law on my father's side." She nodded toward the young man, whose face was as expressionless as sand. "Ralf Hadler. I like to keep him around," She raised her voice. "Ralf, go find the Getabout. It's parked somewhere in back."

The Cohorts, either singly or in bunches, made Allen uncomfortable; they were humorless, as devout as machines, and, for their small number, they seemed to be everywhere. His fantasy was that the Cohorts were always in motion; in the course of one day, like a foraging ant, a member of the Cohorts roamed hundreds of miles.

"You'll come along," Mrs. Frost said to Mavis.

"Naturally," Mavis murmured. He began clearing his desk of unfinished work. Mavis was an ulcer-mongerer, a high-strung worrier with rumpled shirt and baggy, unpressed tweeds, who flew into fragments when things got over his head. Allen recalled tangled interviews that had ended with Mavis in despair and his staff scurrying. If Mavis was going to be along, the next few hours would be hectic.

"We'll meet you at the Getabout," Mrs. Frost said to him. "Finish up here, first. We'll wait."

As she and Allen walked down the hall, Allen observed: "This is a big place." The idea of an organ—even a government organ—occupying an entire building struck him as grandiose. And much of it was underground. Telemedia, like cleanliness, was next to God; after T-M came the secretaries and the Committee itself.

"It's big," Mrs. Frost agreed, striding along the hall and holding her manila folder against her chest with both hands. "But I don't know."

"You don't know what?"

Cryptically, she said: "Maybe it should be smaller. Remember what became of the giant reptiles."

"You mean curtail its activities?" He tried to picture the vacuum that would be created. "And what instead?"

"Sometimes I toy with the idea of slicing T-M into a number of units, interacting, but separately run. I'm not sure one person can or should take responsibility for the whole."

"Well," Alan said, thinking of Mavis, "I suppose it cuts into his life-expectancy."

"Myron has been Director of T-M for eight years. He's forty-two and he looks eighty. He's got only half a stomach. Someday I expect to phone and discover he's holed up at the Health Resort, doing business from there. Or from Other World, as they call that sanitarium of theirs."

"That's a long way off," Allen said. "Either place."

They had come to the door leading out, and Mrs. Frost halted. "You've been in a position to watch T-M. What do you think of it? Be honest with me. Would you call it efficient?"

"The part I see is efficient."

"What about the output? It buys your packets and it frames them for a medium. What's your reaction to the end result? Is the Morec garbled along the line? Do you feel your ideas survive projection?"

Allen tried to recall when he had last sat through a T-M concoction. His Agency monitored as a matter of routine, collecting its own duplicates of the items based on its packets. "Last week," he said, "I watched a television show."

The woman's gray eyebrows lifted mockingly. "Half hour? Or entire hour?"

"The program was an hour but we saw only a portion of it. At a friend's apartment. Janet and I were over playing Juggle, and we were taking a break."

"You don't mean you don't own a television set."

"The people downstairs are domino for my block. They tumble the rest of us. Apparently the packets are getting over."

They walked outside and got into the parked Getabout. Allen calculated that this zone, in terms of leasing, was in the lowest possible range: between 1 and 14. It was not crowded.

"Do you approve of the domino method?" Mrs. Frost asked as they waited for Mavis.

"It's certainly economical."

"But you have reservations."

"The domino method operates on the assumption that people believe what their group believes, no more and no less. One unique individual would foul it up. One man who originated his own idea, instead of getting it from his block domino."

Mrs. Frost said: "How interesting. An idea out of nothing."

"Out of the individual human mind," Allen said, aware that he wasn't being political, but feeling, at the same time, that Mrs. Frost respected him and really wanted to hear what he had to offer. "A rare situation," he admitted. "But it could occur."

There was a stir outside the car. Myron Mavis, a bulging briefcase under his arm, and the Cohort of Major Streiter, his young face stern and his messenger parcel chained to his belt, had arrived.

"I forgot about you," Mrs. Frost said to her cousin, as the two men got in. The Getabout was small, and there was barely room for all of them. Hadler was to drive. He started up the motor — powered by pile-driven steam — and the car moved cautiously along the lane. Along the route to the Committee building, they passed only three other Getabouts.

"Mr. Purcell has a criticism of the domino method," Mrs. Frost said to Myron Mavis.

Mavis grunted unintelligibly, then blinked bloodshot eyes and roused himself. "Uhuh," he muttered. "Fine." He began pawing through a pocketful of papers. "Let's go back to five-minute spots. Hit 'em, hit 'em."

Behind the tiller, young Hadler sat very straight and rigid, his chin out-jutting. He gripped the tiller as a person walked across the lane ahead. The Getabout had reached a speed of twenty miles an hour, and all four of them were uneasy.

"We should either fly," Mavis grated, "or walk. Not this half-way business. All we need now is a couple of bottles of beer, and we're back in the old days."

"Mr. Purcell believes in the unique individual," Mrs. Frost said.

Mavis favored Allen with a glance. "The Resort has that on its mind, too. An obsession, day and night."

"I always assumed that was window dressing," Mrs. Frost said. "To lure people into going over."

"People go over because they're noose," Mavis declared. *Noose* was a derisive term contracted from *neuro-psychiatric*. Allen disliked it. It had a blind, savage quality that made him think of the old hate terms, *nigger* and *kike*. "They're weak, they're misfits, they can't take it. They haven't got the moral fiber to stick it out here; like babies, they want pleasure. They want candy and bottled pop. Comic books from mama Health Resort."

On his face was an expression of great bitterness. The bitterness was like a solvent that had eaten through the wasted folds of flesh, exposing the bone. Allen had never seen Mavis so weary and discouraged.

"Well," Mrs. Frost said, also noticing, "we don't want them anyway. It's better they should go over."

"I sometimes wonder what they do with all those people," Allen said. Nobody had accurate figures on the number of renegades who had fled to the Resort; because of the onus, the relatives preferred to state that the missing individual had gone to the colonies. Colonists were, after all, only failures; a noose was a voluntary expatriate who had declared himself an enemy of moral civilization.

"I've heard," Mrs. Frost said conversationally, "that incoming supplicants are set to work in vast slave-labor camps. Or was that the Communists who did that?"

"Both," Allen said. "And with the revenue, the Resort is building a vast empire in outer space to dominate the universe. Huge robot armies, too. Women supplicants are —" He concluded briefly: "Ill-used."

At the tiller of the Getabout, Ralf Hadler said suddenly: "Mrs. Frost, there's a car behind us trying to pass. What'll I do?"

"Let it pass." They all looked around. A Getabout, like their own, but with the sticker of the Pure Food and Drug League, was nosing its way to their left side. Hadler had gone white at this unforeseen dilemma, and their Getabout was veering witlessly.

"Pull over and stop," Allen told him.

"Speed up," Mavis said, turning in his seat and peering defiantly through the rear window. "They don't own this lane."

The Pure Food and Drug League Getabout continued to advance on them, equally uncertain of itself. As Hadler dribbled toward the right, it abruptly seized what seemed to be its chance and shot forward. Hadler then let his tiller slide between his hands, and two fenders scraped shatteringly.

Mavis, trembling, crept from their stopped Getabout. Mrs. Frost followed him, and Allen and young Hadler got out on the other side. The Pure Food and Drug League car idled its motor, and the driver — alone inside — gaped out at them. He was a middle-aged gentleman, obviously at the end of a long day at the office.

"Maybe we could back up," Mrs. Frost said, holding her manila folder aimlessly. Mavis, reduced to impotence, wandered around the two Getabouts and poked here and there with his toe. Hadler stood like iron, betraying no feeling.

The fenders had combined, and one car would have to be jacked up. Allen inspected the damage, noted the angle at which the two metals had met, and then gave up. "They have tow trucks," he said to Mrs. Frost. "Have Ralf call the Transportation Pool." He looked around him; they were not far from the Committee building. "We can walk from here."

Without protest, Mrs. Frost started off, and he followed.

"What about me?" Mavis demanded, hurrying a few steps.

"You can stay with the car," Mrs. Frost said. Hadler had already strode toward a building and phone booth; Mavis was alone with the gentleman from the Pure Food and Drug League. "Tell the police what happened."

A cop, on foot, was walking over. Not far behind him came a juvenile, attracted by the convocation of people.

"This embarrassing is," Mrs. Frost said presently, as the two of them walked toward the Committee building.

"I suppose Ralf will go up before his block warden." The picture of Mrs. Birmingham entered his mind, the coyly sweet malevolence of the creature situated behind her table, dealing out trouble.

Mrs. Frost said: "The Cohorts have their own inquiry setup." As they reached the front entrance of the building, she said thoughtfully: "Mavis is completely burned out. He can't cope with any situation. He makes no decisions. Hasn't for months."

Allen didn't comment. It wasn't his place.

"Maybe it's just as well," Mrs. Frost said. "Leaving him back there. I'd rather see Mrs. Hoyt without him trailing along."

This was the first he had heard that they were meeting with Ida Pease Hoyt. Halting, he said: "Maybe you should explain what you're going to do."

"I believe you know what I'm going to do," she said, continuing on.

And he did.

4

ALLEN PURCELL RETURNED home to his one-room apartment at the hour of nine-thirty p.m. Janet met him at the door.

"Did you eat?" she asked. "You didn't."

"No," he admitted, entering the room.

"I'll fix you something." She set back the wall tape and restored the kitchen, which had departed at eight. In a few minutes, "Alaskan salmon" was baking in the oven, and the near-authentic odor drifted through the room. Janet put on an apron and began setting the table.

Throwing himself down on a chair, Allen opened the evening paper. But he was too tired to read; he changed his mind and pushed the paper away. The meeting with Ida Pease Hoyt and Sue Frost had lasted three hours. It had been grueling.

"Do you want to tell me what happened?" Janet asked.

"Later." He fooled with a sugar cube at the table. "How was the Book Club? Sir Walter Scott written anything good lately?"

"Not a thing," she said shortly, responding to the tone of his voice.

"You believe Charles Dickens is here to stay?"

She turned from the stove. "Something happened and I want to know what it is."

Her concern made him relent. "The Agency was *not* exposed as a vice den."

"You said on the phone you went to T-M. And you said something terrible happened at the Agency."

"I fired Fred Luddy, if you call that terrible. When'll the 'salmon' be ready?"

"Soon. Five minutes."

Allen said: "Ida Pease Hoyt offered me Mavis' job. Director of Telemedia. Sue Frost did all the talking."

For a moment Janet stood at the stove and then she began to cry.

"Why the heck are you crying?" Allen demanded.

Between sobs she choked: "I don't know. I'm scared."

He went on fooling with the sugar cube. Now it had broken in half, so he flattened the halves to grains. "It wasn't much of a surprise. The post is always filled from the Agencies, and Mavis has been washed up for months. Eight years is a long time to be responsible for everybody's morality."

"Yes, you—said—he should retire." She blew her nose and rubbed her eyes. "Last year you told me that."

"Trouble is, he really wants to do the job."

"Does he know?"

"Sue Frost told him. He finished up the meeting. The four of us sat around drinking coffee and settling it."

"Then it *is* settled?"

Thinking of the look on Mavis' face when he left the meeting, Allen said: "No. Not completely. Mavis resigned; his paper is in, and Sue's statement has gone out. The routine protocol. Years of devoted service, faithful adherence to the Principles of Moral Reclamation. I talked to him briefly in the hall afterward." Actually, he had walked a quarter mile with Mavis, from the Committee building to Mavis' apartment. "He's got a piece of planet in the Sirius System. They're great on cattle. According to Mavis, you can't distinguish the taste and texture from the domestic herds."

Janet said: "What's undecided?"

"Maybe I won't take it."

"Why not?"

"I want to be alive eight years from now. I don't want to be retiring to some God-forsaken rustic backwater ten light years away."

Pushing her handkerchief into her breast pocket, Janet bent to turn off the oven. "Once, when we were setting up the Agency, we talked about this. We were very frank."

"What did we decide?" He remembered what they had decided. They decided to decide when the time came, because it might very well never come. And anyhow Janet was too busy worrying about the imminent collapse of the Agency. "This is all so useless. We're acting as if the job is some sort of plum. It's not a plum and it never was. Nobody ever pretended it was. Why did Mavis take it? Because it seemed like the moral thing to do."

"Public service," Janet said faintly.

"The moral responsibility to serve. To take on the burden on civic life. The highest form of self-sacrifice, the *omphalos* of this whole —" He broke off.

"Rat race," Janet said. "Well, there'll be a little more money. Or does it pay less? I guess that isn't important."

Allen said: "My family has climbed a long way. I've done some climbing, too. This is what it's for; this is the goal. I'd like a buck for every packet I've done on the subject." The packet Sue Frost had returned, in fact. The parable about the tree that died.

The tree had died in isolation, and perhaps the Morec of the packet was confused and obscure. But to him it came over clearly enough: a man was primarily responsible to his fellows, and it was with his fellows that he made his life.

"There're two men," he said. "Squatting in the ruins, off in Hokkaido. That place is contaminated. Everything's dead, there. They have one future; they're waiting for it. Gates and Sugermann would rather be dead than come back here. If they came back here they'd have to become social beings; they'd have to sacrifice some part of their ineffable selves. And that is certainly an awful thing."

"That's not the only reason why they're out there," Janet said, in a voice so low that he could barely hear her. "I guess you've forgotten. I've been there, too. You took me with you, one time. When we were first married. I wanted to see."

He remembered. But it didn't seem important. "Probably it's a protest of some sort. They have some point they want to make, camping there in the ruins."

"They're giving up their lives."

"That doesn't take any effort. And somebody can always save them with quick-freeze."

"But in dying they make an important point. Don't you think so? Maybe not." She reflected. "Myron Mavis made a point, too. Not a very different point. And you must see something in what Gates and Sugermann are doing; you keep going out there again and again. You were there last night."

He nodded. "I was."

"What did Mrs. Birmingham say?"

Without particular emotion he answered: "A juvenile saw me, and I'm down for Wednesday's block meeting."

"Because you went there? They never reported it before."

"Maybe they never saw me before."

"Do you know about afterward? Did the juvenile see that?"

"Let's hope not," he said.

"It's in the paper."

He snatched up the paper. It was in the paper, and it was on page one. The headlines were large.

STREITER STATUE DESECRATED

VANDALS IN PARK

INVESTIGATION UNDERWAY

"That was you," Janet said tonelessly.

"It was," he agreed. He read the headlines again. "It really was me. And it took an hour to do. I left the paint can on a bench. They probably found it."

"That's mentioned in the article. They noticed the statue this morning around six A.M., and they found the paint can at six-thirty."

"What else did they find?"

"Read it, "Janet said.

Spreading the paper out flat on the table, he read it.

STREITER STATUE DESECRATED

VANDALS IN PARK

INVESTIGATION UNDERWAY

Newer York, Oct. 8 (T-M). Police are investigating the deliberate mutilation of the official statue of Major Jules Streiter, the founder of Moral Reclamation and the guiding leader of the revolution of 1985. Located in the Park of the Spire, the monument, a life-size statue of bronzed plastic, was struck from the original mold created by the founder's friend and lifelong companion, Pietro Buetello in March of the year 1990. The mutilation, described by police as deliberate and systematic, apparently took place during the night. The Park of the Spire is never closed to the public, since it represents the moral and spiritual center of Newer York.

"The paper was downstairs when I got home," Janet said. "As always. With the mail. I read it while I was eating dinner."

"It's easy to see why you're upset."

"Because of that? I'm not upset because of that. All they can do is unease us, fine us, send you to prison for a year."

"And bar our families from Earth."

Janet shrugged. "We'd live. They'd live. I've been thinking about it; I've had three hours and a half here alone in the apartment. At first I was —" She pondered. "Well, it was hard to believe. But this morning we both knew something had happened; there was the mud and grass on your shoes, and the red paint. And nobody saw you."

"A juvenile saw something."

"Not that. They'd have picked you up. It must have seen something else."

Allen said: "I wonder how long it'll be."

"Why should they find out? They'll think it's some person who lost his lease, somebody who's been forced back to the colonies. Or a noose."

"I hate that word."

"A supplicant, then. But why you? Not a man going to the top, a man who spent this afternoon with Sue Frost and Ida Pease Hoyt. It wouldn't make sense."

"No," he admitted. "It doesn't." Truthfully he added: "Even to me."

Janet walked over to the table. "I wondered about that. You're not sure why you did it, are you?"

"I haven't an idea in the world."

"What was in your mind?"

"A very clear desire," he said. "A fixed, overwhelming, and totally clear desire to get that statue once and for all. It took half a gallon of red paint, and some skillful use of a power-driven saw. The saw's back in the Agency shop, minus a blade. I busted the blade. I haven't sawed in years."

"Do you remember precisely what you did?"

"No," he answered.

"It isn't in the paper. They're vague about it. So whatever it was —" She smiled listlessly down at him. "You did a good job."

Later, when the baked "Alaskan salmon" was nothing but a few bones on an empty dinner platter, Allen leaned back and lit a cigarette. At the stove Janet carefully washed pots and pans in the sink attachment. The apartment was peaceful.

"You'd think," Allen said, "this was like any other evening."

"We might as well go on with what we were doing," Janet said.

On the table by the couch was a pile of metal wheels and gears. Janet had been assembling an electric clock. Diagrams and instructions from an Edufacture kit were heaped with the parts. Instructional pastimes: Edufacture for the individual, Juggle for social gatherings. To keep idle hands occupied.

"How's the clock coming?" he asked.

"Almost done. After that comes a shaving wand for you. Mrs. Duffy across the hall made one for her husband. I watched her. It isn't hard."

Pointing to the stove Allen said: "My family built that. Back in 2096, when I was eleven. I remember how silly it seemed; stoves were on sale, built by autofac at a third of the cost. Then my father and brother explained the Morec. I never forgot it."

Janet said: "I enjoy building things; it's fun."

He went on smoking his cigarette, thinking how bizarre it was that he could be here when, less than twenty-four hours ago, he had japed the statue.

"I japed it," he said aloud.

"You —"

"A term we use in packet assembly. When a theme is harped on too much you get parody. When we make fun of a stale theme we say we've japed it."

"Yes," she agreed. "I know. I've heard you parody some of Blake-Moffet's stuff."

"The part that bothers me," Allen said, "is this: On Sunday night I japed the statue of Major Streiter. And on Monday morning Mrs. Sue Frost came to the Agency. By six o'clock I was listening to Ida Pease Hoyt offer me the directorship of Telemedia."

"How could there be a relationship?"

"It would have to be complex." He finished his cigarette. "So roundabout that everybody and everything in the universe would have to be brought in. But I feel it's there. Some deep, underlying causal connection, not chance. Not coincidence."

"Tell me how you — japed it."

"Can't. Don't remember." He got to his feet. "Don't you wait up. I'm going downtown and look at it; they probably haven't had time to start repairs."

Janet said instantly: "Please don't go out."

"Very necessary," he said, looking around for his coat. The closet had absorbed it, and he pulled the closet back into the room. "There's a dim picture in my mind, nothing firm. All things considered, I really should have it clear. Maybe then I can decide about T-M."

Without a word Janet passed by him and out into the hall. She was on her way to the bathroom, and he knew why. With her went a collection of bottles: she was going to swallow enough sedatives to last her the balance of the night.

"Take it easy," he warned.

There was no answer from the closed bathroom door. Allen hung around a moment, and then left.

5

THE PARK WAS in shadows, and icy-dark. Here and there small groups of people had collected like pools of nocturnal rain water. Nobody spoke. They seemed to be waiting, hoping in some vague way for something to happen.

The statue had been erected immediately before the spire, on its own platform, in the center of a gravel ring. Benches surrounded the statue so that persons could feed the pigeons and doze and talk while contemplating its grandeur. The rest of the Park was sloping fields of wet grass, a few opaque humps of shrubs and trees, and, at one end, a gardener's shed.

Allen reached the center of the Park and halted. At first he was confused; nothing familiar was visible. Then he realized what had happened. The police had boarded the statue up. Here was a square wooden frame, a gigantic box. So he wasn't going to see it after all. He wasn't going to find out what he had done.

Presently, as he stood dully staring, he became aware that somebody was beside him. A seedy, spindly-armed citizen in a long, soiled overcoat, was also staring at the box.

For a time neither man spoke. Finally the citizen hawked and spat into the grass. "Sure can't see worth a damn."

Allen nodded.

"They put that up on purpose," the thin citizen said. "So you can't see. You know why?"

"Why," Allen said.

The thin citizen leaned at him. "Anarchists got to it. Mutilated it terribly. The police caught some of them; some they didn't catch. The ringleader, they didn't catch him. But they will. And you know what they'll find?"

"What," Allen said.

"They'll find he's paid by the Resort. And this is just the first."

"Of what?"

"Within the next week," the thin citizen revealed, "public buildings are going to be bombed. The Committee building, T-M. And then they put the radioactive particles in the drinking water. You'll see. It already tastes wrong. The police know, but their hands are tied."

Next to the thin citizen a short, fat, red-haired man smoking a cigar spoke irritably up. "It was kids, that's all. A bunch of crazy kids with nothing else to do."

The thin citizen laughed harshly. "That's what they want you to think. Sure, a harmless prank. I'll tell you something: *the people that did this mean to overthrow Morec.* They won't rest until every scrap of morality and decency has been trampled into the ground. They want to see fornication and neon signs and dope come back. They want to see waste and rapacity rule sovereign, and vainglorious man writhe in the sinkpit of his own greed."

"It was kids," the short fat man repeated. "Doesn't mean anything."

"The wrath of Almighty God will roll up the heavens like a scroll," the thin citizen was telling him, as Allen walked off. "The atheists and fornicators will lie bloody in the streets, and the evil will be burned from men's hearts by the sacred fire."

By herself, hands in the pockets of her coat, a girl watched Allen as he walked aimlessly along the path. He approached her, hesitated, and then said: "What happened?"

The girl was dark-haired, deep-chested, with smooth, tanned skin that glowed faintly in the half-light of the Park. When she spoke her voice was controlled and without uncertainty. "This morning they found the statue to be quite different. Didn't you read about it? There was an account in the newspaper."

"I read about it," he said. The girl was up on a rise of grass, and he joined her.

There, in the shadows below them, were the remnants of the statue, damaged in a cunning way. The image of bronzed plastic had been caught unguarded; in the night it had been asleep. Standing here now he could take an objective view; he could detach himself from the event and see it as an outsider, as a person — like these persons — coming by accident, and wondering.

Across the gravel were large ugly drops of red. It was the enamel from the art department of his Agency. But he could suppose the apocalyptic quality of it; he could imagine what these people imagined.

The trail of red was blood, the statue's blood. Up from the wet, loose-packed soil of the Park had crept its enemy; the enemy had taken hold and bitten through its carotid artery. The statue had bled all over its own legs and feet; it had gushed red slimy blood and died.

He, standing with the girl, knew it was dead. He could feel the emptiness behind the wooden box; the blood had run out leaving a hollow container. It seemed now as if the statue had tried to defend itself. But it had lost, and no quick-freeze would save it. The statue was dead forever.

"How long have you been here?" the girl asked.

"Just a couple of minutes," he said.

"I was here this morning. I saw it on my way to work."

Then he realized, she had seen it before the box was erected. "What did they do to it?" he asked, earnestly eager to find out. "Could you tell?"

The girl said: "Don't be scared."

"I'm not scared." He was puzzled.

"You are. But it's all right." She laughed. "Now they'll have to take it down. They can't repair it."

"You're glad," he said, awed.

The girl's eyes filled with light, a rocking amusement. "We should celebrate. Have ourselves a ball." Then her eyes faded. "If he can get away with it, whoever he was, whoever did it. Let's get out of here — okay? Come on."

She led him across the grass to the sidewalk and the lane beyond. Hands in her pockets, she walked rapidly along, and he followed. The night air was chilly and sharp, and, gradually, it cleared from his mind the mystical dream-like presence of the Park.

"I'm glad to get out of there," he murmured finally.

With an uneasy toss of her head the girl said: "It's easy to go in there, hard to get out."

"You felt it?"

"Of course. It wasn't so bad this morning, when I walked by. The sun was shining; it was daylight. But tonight—" She shivered. "I was there an hour before you came and woke me up. Just standing, looking at it. In a trance."

"What got me," he said, "were those drops. They looked like blood."

"Just paint," she answered matter-of-factly. Reaching into her coat she brought out a folded newspaper. "Want to read? A common fast-drying enamel, used by a lot of offices. Nothing mysterious about it."

"They haven't caught anybody," he said, still feeling some of the unnatural detachment. But it was departing.

"Surprising how easily a person can do this and get away. Why not? Nobody guards the Park; nobody actually saw him."

"What's your theory?"

"Well," she said, kicking a bit of rock ahead of her. "Somebody was bitter about losing his lease. Or somebody was expressing a subconscious resentment of Morec. Fighting back against the burden the system imposes."

"Exactly what was done to the statue?"

"The paper didn't print the details. It's probably safer to play a thing like this down. You've seen the statue; you're familiar with the Buetello conception of Streiter. The traditional militant stance: one hand extended, one leg forward as if he were going into battle. Head up nobly. Deeply thoughtful expression."

"Looking into the future," Allen murmured.

"That's right." The girl slowed down, spun on her heel and peered at the dark pavement. "The criminal, or japer, or whatever he is, painted the statue red. You know that; you saw the drops. He sloshed it with stripes, painted the hair red, too. And —" She smiled brightly. "Well, frankly, he severed the head, somehow. With a power cutting tool, evidently. Removed the head and placed it in the outstretched hand."

"I see," Allen said, listening intently.

"Then," the girl continued, in a quiet monotone, "the individual applied a high-temperature pack to the forward leg — the right leg. The statue is a poured thermoplastic. When the leg became flexible, the culprit reshaped its position. Major Streiter now appears to be holding his head in his hand, ready to kick it far into the park. Quite original, and *quite* embarrassing."

After an interval Allen said: "Under the circumstances you can't blame them for nailing a box around it."

"They had to. But a number of people saw it before they put the box up. The first thing they did was get the Cohorts of Major

Streiter over; they must have thought something else was going to happen. When I went by, there were all those sullen-looking young men in their brown uniforms, a ring of them around the statue. But you could see anyhow. Then, sometime during the day, they put up the box." She added: "You see, people laughed. Even the Cohorts. They couldn't help it. They snickered, and then it got away from them. I was so sorry for those young men ... they hated to laugh so."

Now the two of them had reached a lighted intersection. The girl halted. On her face was an expression of concern. She gazed up at him intently, studying him, her eyes large.

"You're in a terrible state," she said. "And it's my fault."

"No," he answered. "My own fault."

Her hand pressed against his arm. "What's wrong?"

With irony he said: "Job worries."

"Oh." She nodded. But she still held onto his arm with her tight fingers. "Well, do you have a wife?"

"A very sweet one."

"Does she help you?"

"She worries even more than I. Right now she's home taking pills. She has a fabulous collection."

The girl said: "Do you want help?"

"I do," he answered, and was not surprised at his own candor. "Very much."

"That's what I thought." The girl began to walk on, and he went along. She seemed to be weighing various possibilities. "These days," she said, "it's hard to get help. You're not supposed to *want* help. I can give you an address. If I do, will you use it?"

"That's impossible to say."

"Will you *try* to use it?"

"I've never asked for help in my life," Allen said. "I can't say what I'd do."

"Here it is," the girl said. She handed him a slip of folded pa-per. "Put it away in your wallet. "Don't look at it — just put it away until you want to use it. Then get it out."

He put it away, and she watched fixedly.

"All right," she said, satisfied. "Good night."

"You're leaving?" He wasn't surprised; it seemed perfectly natural.

"I'll see you again. I've seen you before." She dwindled in the darkness of the side lane. "Good night, Mr. Purcell. Take care of yourself."

Sometime later, after the girl was completely gone, he real-ized that she had been standing there in the Park waiting for him. Waiting, because she knew he would show up.

6

THE NEXT DAY Allen had still not given Mrs. Frost an answer. The directorship of T-M was empty, with Mavis out and nobody in. The huge trust rolled along on momentum; and, he supposed, minor bureaucrats along the line continued to stamp forms and fill out papers. The monster lived, but not as it should.

Wondering how long he had to decide he phoned the Committee building and asked for Mrs. Frost.

"Yes sir," a recorded voice answered. "Secretary Frost is in conference. You may state a thirty-second message which will be transcribed for her attention. Thank you. Zeeeeeeeeeeeee!"

"Mrs. Frost," Allen said, "there are a number of considerations involved, as I mentioned to you yesterday. Heading an Agency gives me a certain independence. You pointed out that my only customer is Telemedia, so that for all practical purposes I'm working for Telemedia. You also pointed out that as Director of Telemedia I would have more, not less, independence."

He paused, wondering how to go on.

"On the other hand," he said, and then the thirty seconds was up. He waited as the mechanism at the other end repeated its rigamarole, and then continued. "My Agency, after all, was built up by my own hands. I'm free to alter it. I have complete control. T-M, on the other hand, is impersonal. Nobody can really dictate to it. T-M is like a glacier."

That sounded terrible to him, but once on the tape it couldn't be unspoken. He finished up:

"Mrs. Frost, I'm afraid I'll have to have time to think it over. I'm sorry, because I realize this puts you in an unpleasant position. But I'm afraid the delay unavoidable is. I'll try to have my answer within a week, and please don't think I'm stalling. I'm sincerely floundering. This is Allen Purcell."

Ringing off, he sat back and brooded.

Here, in his office, the statue of Major Streiter seemed distant and unconvincing. He had one problem only: the job problem. Either he stayed with his Agency or he went upstairs to T-M. Put that way his dilemma sounded simple. He got out a coin and rolled it across the surface of his desk. If necessary he could leave the decision to chance.

The door opened and Doris, his secretary, entered. "Good morning," she said brightly. "Fred Luddy wants a letter of recommendation from you. We made out his check. Two weeks, plus what was owed." She seated herself across from him, pad and pencil ready. "Do you want to dictate a letter?"

"That's hard to say." He wanted to, because he liked Luddy and he hoped to see him get a halfway decent job. But at the same time he felt silly writing a letter of recommendation for a man he had fired as disloyal and dishonest, Morecly speaking. "Maybe I'll have to think about that, too."

Doris arose. "I'll tell him you're too busy. You'll have to see about it later."

Relieved, he let her go with that story. No decision seemed possible right now, on any topic. Small or large, his problems revolved on an olympian level; they couldn't be hauled down to earth.

At least the police hadn't traced him. He was reasonably

sure that Mrs. Birmingham's juvenile lacked information on the Park episode. Tomorrow, at nine A.M., he'd find out. But he wasn't worried. The idea of police barging in to arrest and deport him was absurd. His real worry was the job — and himself.

He had told the girl he needed help, and he did. Not because he had japed the statue, but because he had japed it without understanding why. Odd that the brain could function on its own, without acquainting him with its purposes, its reasons. But the brain was an organ, like the spleen, heart, kidneys. And they went about their private activities. So why not the brain? Reasoned out that way, the bizarre quality evaporated.

But he still had to find out what was happening.

Reaching into his wallet he got out the slip of paper. On it, in a woman's neat hand, were four words.

Health Resort

Gretchen Malparto.

So the girl's name was Gretchen. And, as he had inferred, she was roaming around in the night soliciting for the Mental Health Resort, in violation of law.

The Health Resort, the last refuge for deserters and misfits, had reached out and put its hand on his shoulder.

He felt weak. He felt very morbid and shaky, as if he were running a fever, a low current of somewhat moist energy that could not be shaken off.

"Mr. Purcell," Doris' voice came through the open door. "There's a return call in for you. The phone is taking it right now."

"Okay, Doris," he said. With effort he roused himself from his thoughts and reached to snap on the phone. The tape obligingly skipped back and restarted itself, spewing the recorded call.

"Ten-o-five. Click. Zeeeeeeeeeeeee! Mr. Purcell." Now a smooth, urbane female voice appeared. With further pessimism he recognized it. "This is Mrs. Sue Frost, answering your call of earlier this morning. I'm sorry I was not in when you called, Mr. Purcell." A pause. "I am fully sympathetic with your situation. I can easily understand the position you're in." Another pause, this one somewhat longer. "Of course, Mr. Purcell, you surely must realize that the offer of the directorship was predicated on the assumption that you were available for the job."

The mechanism jumped to its next thirty-second segment.

"Ten-o-six. Click. Zeeeeeeeeeeeee! To go on." Mrs. Frost cleared her throat. "It strikes us that a week is rather a long time, in view of the difficult status of Telemedia. There is no acting Director, since, as you're aware, Mr. Mavis has already resigned. We hesitate to request a postponement of that resignation, but perhaps it will be necessary. Our suggestion is that you take until Saturday at the latest to decide. Understand, we're fully sympathetic with your situation, and we don't wish to rush you. But Telemedia is a vital trust, and it would be in the public interest that your decision come as quickly as possible. I'll expect to hear from you, then."

Click, the mechanism went. The rest of the tape was blank.

From the tone of Mrs. Frost's message Allen inferred that he had got an official statement of the Committee's position. He could imagine the tape being played back at an inquiry. It was for the record, and then some. Four point five days, he thought. Four point five days to decide what he was and what he ought to be.

Picking up the phone, he started to dial, then changed his mind. Calling from the Agency was too risky. Instead, he left the office.

"Going out again, Mr. Purcell?" Doris asked, at her own desk.

"I'll be back shortly. Going over to the commissary for some supplies." He tapped his coat pocket. "Things Janet asked me to pick up."

As soon as he was out of the Mogentlock Building he stepped into a public phone booth. Staring vacantly, he dialed.

"Mental Health Resort," a bureaucratic, but friendly voice answered in his ear.

"Is there a Gretchen Malparto there?"

Time passed. "Miss Malparto has left the Resort temporarily. Would you like to speak to Doctor Malparto?"

Obscurely nettled, Allen said: "Her husband?"

"Doctor Malparto is Miss Malparto's brother. Who is calling, please?"

"I want an appointment," Allen said. "Business problems."

"Yes sir." The rustle of papers. "Your name, sir?"

He hesitated and then invented. "I'll be in under the name Coates."

"Yes sir, Mr. Coates." There was no further questioning on that point. "Would tomorrow at nine A.M. be satisfactory?"

He started to agree, and then remembered the block meeting. "Better make it Thursday."

"Thursday at nine," the girl said briskly. "With Doctor Malparto. Thank you very much for calling."

Feeling a little better, Allen returned to the Agency.

7

IN THE HIGHLY moral society of 2114 A.D., the weekly block meetings operated on the stagger system. Wardens from surrounding housing units were able to sit at each, forming a board of which the indigenous warden was chairman. Since Mrs. Birmingham was the warden in the Purcells' block, she, of the assembled middle-aged ladies, occupied the raised seat. Her compatriots, in flowered silk dresses, filled chairs on each side of her across the platform.

"I hate this room," Janet said, pausing at the door.

Allen did, too. Down here on the first level of the housing unit, in this one large chamber, all the local Leagues, Committees, Clubs, Boards, Associations, and Orders met. The room smelled of stale sunlight, dust, and the infinite layers of paperwork that had piled up over the years. Here, official nosing and snooping originated. In this room a man's business was everybody's business. Centuries of Christian confessional culminated when the block assembled to explore its members' souls.

As always, there were more people than space. Many had to stand, and they filled the corners and aisles. The air conditioning system moaned and reshuffled the cloud of smoke. Allen was always puzzled by the smoke, since nobody seemed to have a cigarette and smoking was forbidden. But there it was. Perhaps it, like the shadow of purifying fire, was an accumulation from the past.

His attention fixed itself on the pack of juveniles. They were here, the earwig-like sleuths. Each juvenile was a foot and a half long. The species scuttled close to the ground — or up vertical surfaces — at ferocious speed, and they noticed everything. These juveniles were inactive. The wardens had unlocked the metal hulls and dug out the report tapes. The juveniles remained inert during the meeting, and then they were put back into service.

There was something sinister in these metal informers, but there was also something heartening. The juveniles did not accuse; they only reported what they heard and saw. They couldn't color their information and they couldn't make it up. Since the victim was indicted mechanically he was safe from hysterical hearsay, from malice and paranoia. But there could be no question of guilt; the evidence was already in. The issue to be settled here was merely the severity of moral lapse. The victim couldn't protest that he had been unjustly accused; all he could protest was his bad luck at having been overheard.

On the platform Mrs. Birmingham held the agenda and looked to see if everybody had arrived. Failure to arrive was in itself a lapse. Apparently he and Janet completed the group; Mrs. Birmingham signalled, and the meeting began.

"I guess we don't get to sit," Janet murmured, as the door closed after them. Her face was pinched with anxiety; for her the weekly block meeting was a catastrophe which she met with hopelessness and despair. Each week she anticipated denouncement and downfall, but it never came. Years had gone by, and she had still not officially erred. But that only convinced her that doom was saving itself up for one grand spree.

"When they call me," Allen said softly, "you keep your mouth shut. Don't get in on either side. The less said the better chance I have."

She glared at him with suffering. "They'll tear you apart. Look at them." She swept in the whole room. "They're just waiting to get at somebody."

"Most of them are bored and wish they were out." As a matter of fact, several men were reading their morning newspapers. "So take it easy. If nobody leaps to defend me it'll die down and maybe I'll get off with a verbal reprimand." Assuming, of course, that nothing was in about the statue.

"We will first undertake the case of Miss J. E.," Mrs. Birmingham stated. Miss J. E. was Julie Ebberley, and everybody in the room knew her. Julie had been up time and again, but somehow she managed to hang onto the lease willed her by her family. Scared and wide-eyed, she now mounted the defendant's stage, a young blonde-haired girl with long legs and an intriguing bosom. Today she wore a modest print dress and low-heeled slippers. Her hair was tied back in a girlish knot.

"Miss J. E.," Mrs. Birmingham declared, "did willingly and knowingly on the night of October 6, 2114, engage with a man in a vile enterprise."

In most cases a "vile enterprise" was sex. Allen half-closed his eyes and prepared to endure the session. A shuffling murmur ran through the room; the newspapers were put aside. Apathy dwindled. To Allen this was the offensive part: the leering need to hear a confession down to the last detail — a need which masqueraded as righteousness.

The first question came instantly. "Was this the same man as the other times?"

Miss J. E. colored. "Y-Yes," she admitted.

"Weren't you warned? Hadn't you been told in this very room to get yourself home at a decent hour and act like a good girl?"

In all probability that was now a different questioner. The

voice was synthetic, issuing from a wall speaker. To preserve
the aura of justice, questions were piped through a common
channel, broken down and reassembled without characteristic timbre. The result was an impersonal accuser, who, when a
sympathetic questioner appeared, became suddenly and a little
oddly a defender.

"Let's hear what this 'vile enterprise' was," Allen said, and, as
always, was revolted to hear his voice boom out dead and char-
acterless. "This may be a furor about nothing."

On the platform Mrs. Birmingham peered distastefully down,
seeking to identify the questioner. Then she read from the summary. "Miss J. E. did willingly in the bathtub of the community
bathroom of her housing unit — this unit — copulate."

"I'd call that something," the voice said, and then the dogs
were loose. The accusations fell thick and fast, a blur of lascivi-
ous racket.

Beside Allen his wife huddled against him. He could feel her
dread and he put his arm around her. In a while the voice would
be tearing at him.

At nine-fifteen the faction vaguely defending Miss J. E.
seemed to have gained an edge. After a conference the council
of block wardens released the girl with an oral reprimand, and
she slipped gratefully from the room. Mrs. Birmingham again
arose with the agenda.

With relief Allen heard his own initials. He walked forward,
listening to the charges, glad to get it over with. The juvenile —
thank God — had reported about as expected.

"Mr. A. P.," Mrs. Birmingham declared, "did on the night of
October 7, 2114, at 11:30 P.M., arrive home in a drunken state and
did fall on the front steps of the housing unit and in so doing utter a morally objectionable word."

Allen climbed the stage, and the session began.

· · ·

There was always the danger that somewhere in the room a citizen waited with a deeply-buried quirk, a deposit of hate nourished and hoarded for just such an occasion as this. During the years that he had leased in this housing unit Allen might easily have slighted some nameless soul; the human mind being what it was, he might have set off a tireless vengeance by stepping ahead in line, failing to nod, treading on foot, or the like.

But as he looked around he saw no special emotion. Nobody glowered demonically, and nobody, except for his stricken wife, even appeared interested.

Considering the shallowness of the charge he had good reason to feel optimistic. All in all, he was well off. Realizing this, he faced his composite accuser cheerfully.

"Mr. Purcell," it said, "you haven't been up before us in quite a spell." It corrected: "Mr. A. P., I meant."

"Not for several years," he answered.

"How much had you had to drink?"

"Three glasses of wine."

"And you were drunk on that?" The voice answered itself: "That's the indictment." It haggled, and then a clear question emerged. "Where did you get drunk?"

Not wishing to volunteer material, Allen kept his answer brief. "At Hokkaido." Mrs. Birmingham was aware of that, so evidently it didn't matter.

"What were you doing there?" the voice asked, and then it said: "That's not relevant. That has nothing to do with it. Stick to the facts. What he did before he was drunk doesn't matter."

To Allen it sounded like Janet. He let it battle on.

"Of course it matters. The importance of the act depends on the motives behind it. Did he mean to get drunk? Nobody *means* to get drunk. I'm sure I wouldn't know."

Allen said: "It was on an empty stomach, and I'm not used to liquor in any form."

"What about the word he used? Yes, what about it? Well, we don't even know what it was. I think we're just as well off. Why, are you convinced he's the sort of man who would use words 'like that'? All I mean is that knowing the particular word doesn't affect the situation."

"And I was tired," Allen added. Years of work with media had taught him the shortest routes to the Morec mind. "Although it was Sunday I had spent the day at the office. I suppose I did more than was good for my health, but I like to have my desk clear on Monday."

"A regular little gentleman," the voice said. It retorted at once: "With manners enough to keep personalities out of this. Bravo," it said. "That's telling him. Probably her." And then, from the chaos of minds, a sharp sentiment took shape. As nearly as Allen could tell, it was one person. "This a mockery is. Mr. Purcell is one of our most distinguished members. As most of us know, Mr. Purcell's Agency supplies a good deal of the material used by Telemedia. Are we supposed to believe that a man involved in the maintenance of society's ethical standards is, himself, morally defective? What does that say about our society in general? This a paradox is. It is just such high-minded men, devoted to public service, who set by their own examples our standards of conduct."

Surprised, Allen peered across the room at his wife. Janet seemed bewildered. And the choice of words was not characteristic of her. Evidently it was somebody else.

"Mr. Purcell's family leased here several decades," the voice continued. "Mr. Purcell was born here. During his lifetime many persons have come and gone. Few of us have maintained a lease as long as he has. How many of us were here in this room before Mr. Purcell? Think that over. The purpose of these sessions is not the humbling of the mighty. Mr. Purcell isn't up there so we can deride and ridicule him. Some of us seem to imagine the more respectable a person is, the more reason to attack him. When we attack Mr. Purcell we attack our better selves. And there's no percentage in that."

Allen felt embarrassed.

"These meetings," the voice went on, "operate on the idea that a man is morally responsible to his community. That's a good idea. But his community is also morally responsible to him. If it's going to ask him to come up and confess his sins, it's got to give him something in return. It's got to give him its respect and support. It should realize that having a citizen like Mr. Purcell up here is a privilege. Mr. Purcell's life is devoted to our welfare and the improvement of our society. If he wants to drink three glasses of wine once in his life and say one morally objectionable word, I think he should be allowed to. It's okay by me."

There was silence. The roomful of people was cowed by piety. Nobody dared speak.

On the stage, Allen sat wishing somebody would attack. His embarrassment had become shame. The eulogizer was making a mistake; he didn't have the full picture.

"Wait a minute," Allen protested. "Let's get one thing straight. What I did was wrong. I haven't got any more right to get drunk and blaspheme than anybody else."

The voice said: "Let's pass on to the next case. There doesn't seem to be anything here."

On the platform the middle-aged ladies conferred, and presently composed their verdict. Mrs. Birmingham arose.

"The block-neighbors of Mr. A. P. take this opportunity to reprimand him for his conduct of the night of October 7, but feel that in view of his excellent prior record no disciplinary action is indicated. You may step down, Mr. A. P."

Allen stepped down and rejoined his wife. Janet squeezed against him, wildly happy. "Bless him, whoever he was."

"I don't deserve it," Allen said, disturbed.

"You do. Of course you do." Her eyes shone recklessly. "You're a wonderful person."

Not far off, at one of the tables, was a mild little elderly fellow with thinning gray hair and a formal, set smile. Mr. Wales glanced at Allen, then turned immediately away.

"That's the guy," Allen decided. "Wales."

"Are you sure?"

The next accused was up on the stage, and Mrs. Birmingham began reading the indictment. "Mrs. R. M. did knowingly and willingly on the afternoon of October 9, 2114, in a public place and in the presence of both men and women, take the name of the Lord in vain."

The voice said: "What a waste of time." And the controversy was on.

After the meeting Allen approached Wales. The man had lingered outside the door, as if expecting him. Allen had noticed him in the hall a few times, but he didn't recall ever having said more than good morning to him.

"That was you," Allen said.

They shook hands. "I'm glad I could help you out, Mr. Purcell." Wales' voice was drab, perfectly ordinary. "I saw you speak up for that girl. You always look out for the people up there. I said, if he ever gets up I'll do the same for him. We all like and respect you, Mr. Purcell."

"Thanks," Allen said awkwardly.

As he and Janet walked back upstairs, Janet said: "What's the matter?" She was in a delirium at having escaped from the meeting. "Why do you look so glum?"

"I feel glum," he said.

8

DOCTOR MALPARTO SAID: "Good morning, Mr. Coates. Please take off your coat and sit down. I want you to be comfortable."

And then he felt strange and ill, because the man facing him was not "Mr. Coates" but Allen Purcell. Hurriedly getting to his feet Malparto excused himself and went out into the corridor. He was shaking with excitement. Behind him, Purcell looked vaguely puzzled, a tall, good-looking, rather overly-serious man in his late twenties, wearing a heavy overcoat. Here he was, the man Malparto had been expecting. But he hadn't expected him so soon.

With his key he unlocked his file and brought out Purcell's dossier. He glanced over the contents as he returned to his office. The report was as cryptic as before. Here was his prized-gram, and the irreducible syndrome remained. Malparto sighed with delight.

"I beg your pardon, Mr. Purcell," he said, closing the door after him. "Sorry to keep you waiting."

His patient frowned and said: "Let's keep it 'Coates.' Or has that old wheeze about professional confidence gone by the boards?"

"Mr. Coates, then." Malparto reseated himself and put on his glasses. "Mr. Coates, I'll be frank. I've been expecting you. Your encephalogram came into my hands a week or so ago, and I had a Dickson report drawn on it. The profile is unique. I'm very much interested in you, and it's a matter of deep personal satisfaction to be permitted to handle your —" He coughed. "Problem." He had started to say *case*.

In the comfortable leather-covered chair, Mr. Coates shifted restlessly. He lit a cigarette, scowled, rubbed at the crease of his trousers. "I need help. It's one of the drawbacks of Morec that nobody gets help; they get cast out as defective."

Malparto nodded in agreement.

"Also," Mr. Coates said, "your sister came after me."

To Malparto this was discouraging. Not only had Gretchen meddled, but she had meddled wisely. Mr. Coates would have appeared eventually, but Gretchen had sawed the interval in half. He wondered what she got out of it.

"Didn't you know that?" Mr. Coates asked.

He decided to be honest. "No, I didn't. But it's of no consequence." He rattled through the report. "Mr. Coates, I'd like you to tell me in your own words what you feel your problem is."

"Job problems."

"In particular?"

Mr. Coates chewed his lip. "Director of T-M. It was offered to me this Monday."

"You're currently operating an independent Research Agency?" Malparto consulted his notes. "When do you have to decide?"

"By the day after tomorrow."

"Very interesting."

"Isn't it?" Mr. Coates said.

"That doesn't give you long. Do you feel you can decide?"

"No."

"Why not?"

His patient hesitated.

"Are you worried that a juvenile might be hiding in my closet?" Malparto smiled reassuringly. "This is the only spot in our blessed civilization where juveniles are forbidden."

"So I've heard."

"A fluke of history. It seems that Major Streiter's wife had a predilection for psychoanalysts. A Fifth Avenue Jungian cured her partially-paralyzed right arm. You know her type."

Mr. Coates nodded.

"So," Malparto said, "when the Committee Government was set up and the land was nationalized, we were permitted to keep our deeds. We — that is, the Psych Front left over from the war. Streiter was a canny person. Unusual ability. He saw the necessity —"

Mr. Coates said: "Sunday night somebody pulled a switch in my head. So I japed the statue of Major Streiter. That's why I can't accept the T-M directorship."

"Ah," Malparto said, and his eyes fastened on the -gram with its irreducible core. He had a sensation of hanging head downward over an ocean; his lungs seemed filled with dancing foam. Carefully he removed his glasses and polished them with his handkerchief.

Beyond his office window lay the city, flat except for the Morec spire set dead-center. The city radiated in concentric zones, careful lines and swirls that intersected in an orderly manner. Across the planet, Doctor Malparto thought. Like the hide of a vast mammal half-submerged in mud. Half-buried in the drying clay of a stern and puritanical morality.

"You were born here," he said. In his hands was the information, the history of his patient; he leafed through the pages.

"We all were," Mr. Coates said.

"You met your wife in the colonies. What were you doing on Bet-4?"

His patient said: "Supervising a packet. I was consultant to the old Wing-Miller Agency. I wanted a packet rooted in the experience of the agricultural colonists."

"You liked it there?"

"In a way. It was like the frontier. I remember a white-washed board farmhouse. That was her family's . . . her father's." He was quiet a moment. "He and I used to argue. He edited a smalltown newspaper. All night — arguing and drinking coffee."

"Did —" Malparto consulted the dossier. "Did Janet participate?"

"Not much. She listened. I think she was afraid of her father. Maybe a little afraid of me."

"You were twenty-five?"

"Yes," Mr. Coates said. "Janet was twenty-two."

Malparto, reading the information, said: "Your own father was dead. Your mother was alive, still, was she not?"

"She died in 2111," Mr. Coates said. "Not much later."

Malparto put on his video and audio tape transports. "May I keep a record of what we say?"

His patient pondered. "You might as well. You've got me anyhow."

"In my power? Like a wizard? Hardly. I've got your problem; by telling me you've transferred it to me."

Mr. Coates seemed to relax. "Thanks," he said.

"Consciously," Malparto said, "you don't know why you japed the statue; the motive is buried down deep. In all probability the statue episode forms part of a larger event — stretching, perhaps, over years. We'll never be able to understand it alone; its meaning lies in the circumstances preceding it."

His patient grimaced. "You're the wizard."

"I wish you wouldn't think of me like that." He was offended by what he identified as a lay stereotype; the man-in-the-street had come to regard the Resort analysts with a mixture of awe and dread, as if the Resort were a sort of temple and the analysts priests. As if there was some religious mumbo-jumbo involved; whereas, of course, it was all strictly scientific, in the best psychoanalytic tradition.

"Remember, Mr. Coates," he said, "I can only help you if you wish to be helped."

"How much is this going to cost?"

"An examination will be made of your income. You'll be charged according to your ability to pay." It was characteristic of Morec training, this old Protestant frugality. Nothing must be wasted. A hard bargain must always be driven.

The Dutch Reformed Church, alive even in this troubled heretic . . . the power of that iron revolution that had crumbled the Age of Waste, put an end to "sin and corruption," and with it, leisure and peace of mind — the ability simply to sit down and take things easy. How must it have been? he wondered. In the days when idleness was permitted. The golden age, in a sense: but a curious mixture, too, an odd fusion of the liberty of the Renaissance plus the strictures of the Reformation. Both had been there; the two elements struggling in each individual. And, at last, final victory for the Dutch hellfire-preachers . . .

Mr. Coates said: "Let's see some of those drugs you people use. And those light and high-frequency gadgetry."

"In due time."

"Good Lord, I have to tell Mrs. Frost by Saturday!"

Malparto said: "Let's be realistic. No fundamental change can be worked in forty-eight hours. We ran out of miracles several centuries ago. This will be a long, arduous process with many setbacks."

Mr. Coates stirred fitfully.

"You tell me the japery is central," Malparto said. "So let's start there. What were you doing just prior to your entrance into the Park?"

"I visited a couple of friends."

Malparto caught something in his patient's voice, and he said: "Where? Here in Newer York?"

"In Hokkaido."

"Does anybody live there?" He was amazed.

"A few people. They don't live long."

"Have you ever been there before?"

"Now and then. I get ideas for packets."

"And before that. What were you doing?"

"I worked at the Agency most of the day. Then I got—bored."

"You went from the Agency directly to Hokkaido?"

His patient started to nod. And then he stopped, and a dark, intricate expression crossed his face. "No. I walked around for a while. I forgot about that. I remember visiting—" He paused for a long time. "A commissary. To get some 3.2 beer. But why would I want beer? I don't particularly like beer."

"Did anything happen?"

Mr. Coates stared at him. "I can't remember."

Malparto made a notation.

"I left the Agency. And then a haze closes over the whole damn thing. At least half an hour is cut out."

Rising to his feet Malparto pressed a key on his desk intercom. "Would you ask two therapists to step in here, please? And I'm not to be disturbed until further notice. Cancel my next appointment. When my sister comes in I'd like to see her. Yes, let her by. Thanks." He closed the key.

Mr. Coates, agitated, said: "What now?"

"Now you get your wish." Unlocking the supply closet he began wheeling out equipment. "The drugs and gadgetry. So we can dig down and find out what happened between the time you left the Agency and the time you reached Hokkaido."

9

THE SILENCE DEPRESSED him. He was alone in the Mo-gentlock Building, working in the center of a vast tomb. Outside, the sky was cloudy and overcast. At eight-thirty he gave up.

Eight-thirty. Not ten.

Closing his desk he left the Agency and went out onto the dark sidewalk. Nobody was in sight. The lanes were deserted; on Sunday evening there was no flood of commuters. He saw only the shapes of housing units, closed-up commissaries, the hostile sky.

His historical research had acquainted him with the vanished phenomenon of the neon sign. Now he would have wished for a few to break the monotony. The garish, blaring racket of commercials, ads, blinking signs — it had disappeared. Swept aside like a bundle of faded circus posters: to be pulped by history for the printing of textbooks.

Ahead, as he walked sightlessly along the lane, was a cluster of lights. The cluster drew him, and presently he found himself at an autofac receiving station.

The lights formed a hollow ring rising a few hundred feet. Within the circle an autofac ship was lowering itself, a tubby cylinder pitted and corroded by its trip. There were no humans aboard, and there were none at its point of origin. Nor was the receiving equipment manual. When the robot controls had landed the ship, other self-regulating machines would unload it, check the shipment, cart the boxes into the commissary, and store them. Only with the clerk and the customer did the human element come into it.

At the moment a small band of sidewalk superintendents was gathered around the station, following operations. As usual, the bulk of watchers were teen-agers. Hands in their pockets, the boys gazed up raptly. Time passed and none of them stirred. None of them spoke. Nobody came and nobody went.

"Big," one boy finally observed. He was tall, with dull red hair, pebbled skin. "The ship."

"Yes," Allen agreed, also looking up. "I wonder where it's from," he said awkwardly. As far as he was concerned the industrial process was like the movement of planets: it functioned automatically and that was as it should be.

"It's from Bellatrix 7," the boy stated, and two of his mute companions nodded. "Tungsten products. They have been unloading light-globes all day. Bellatrix's only a slave system. None of them habitable."

"Nuts to Bellatrix," a companion spoke up.

Allen was puzzled. "Why?"

"Because you can't live there."

"What do you care?"

The boys regarded him with contempt. "Because we're going," one of them croaked finally.

"Where?"

Contempt turned to disgust; the group of boys edged away from him. "*Out.* Where it's open. Where something's going on."

The red-headed boy told him: "On Sirius 9 they grow walnuts. Almost like here. You can't taste the difference. A whole planet of walnut trees. And on Sirius 8 they grow oranges. Only, the oranges died."

"Mealy bug blight," a companion said gloomily. "Got all the oranges."

The red-headed boy said: "I'm personally going to Orionus. There they breed a real pig you can't tell from the original. I defy you to tell the difference; I defy you."

"But that's away from center," Allen said. "Be realistic — it's taken your families decades to lease this close."

"Shit," one of the boys said bitterly, and then they had melted away, leaving Allen to ponder an obvious fact.

Morec wasn't natural. As a way of life it had to be learned. That was the fact, and the unhappiness of the boys was there to remind him.

The commissary, to which the autofac receiving station belonged, was still open. He stepped through the entrance, reaching, as he did so, for his wallet.

"Sure," the invisible clerk said, as the buy card was punched out. "But only the 3.2 stuff. You really want to drink that?" The window displaying the beer bottles glowed along the wall of items. "It's made from hay."

Once, a thousand years ago, he had punched the slot for 3.2 beer and got a fifth of scotch. God knew where it came from. Perhaps it had survived the war, had been discovered by a robot storekeeper and automatically placed in the single official rack. It had never happened again, but he continued to punch the slot, hoping in a wan, childish way. Evidently it was one of the implausible foul-ups that occurred even in the perfect society.

"Refund," he requested, setting the unopened bottle on the counter. "I've changed my mind."

"I told you," the clerk said, and restored Allen's buy card. Allen stood for a moment, empty-handed, his mind flat with futility. Then he walked outside again.

A moment later he was climbing the ramp to the tiny rooftop

field used by the Agency for rush flights. The sliver was parked there, locked up in its shed.

"And that's all?" Malparto asked. He clicked off the overhanging trellis of wires and lenses that had been focused on his patient. "Nothing else happened between the time you left your office and the time you started for Hokkaido?"

"Nothing else." Mr. Coates lay prone on the table, his arms at his sides. Above him the two technicians examined their meters.

"That was the incident you couldn't remember?"

"Yes, the boys at the autofac station."

"You were despondent?"

"I was." Mr. Coates agreed. His voice lacked emotion; under the blanket of drugs his personality had receded to diffusion.

"Why?"

"Because it was unfair."

Malparto saw no point involved; the incident meant nothing to him. He had expected a sensational revelation of murder or copulation or excitement or all three together.

"Let's go on," he said reluctantly. "The Hokkaido episode itself." Then he lingered. "The incident with the boys. You genuinely feel it was crucial?"

"Yes," Mr. Coates said.

Malparto shrugged, and signaled to his technicians to restart the trellis of paraphernalia.

Darkness lay all around. The sliver dropped toward the island below, guiding itself, speaking to itself mechanically. He rested his head against the seat and closed his eyes. The *whoosh* of descent lessened, and, on the signal board, a blue light blinked.

There was no field to locate; all Hokkaido was a field. He

tripped the landing release, and the ship coasted of its own accord across the surface of ash. Eventually the pattern of Sugermann's transmitter was intercepted and the ship changed its course. The pattern led it in and brought it down. With a faint bump and a few rattles the ship eased to a stop. Now the only sound was the hum of batteries recharging.

Allen opened the door and stepped haltingly out. The ash sank under his feet; it was like standing on mush. The ash was complicated, a mixture of organic and inorganic compounds. A fusion of people and their possessions into a common gray-black blur. During the postwar years the ash had made good mortar.

To his right was an insignificant glow. He walked toward it, and ultimately it became Tom Gates waving a flashlight.

"Morec to you," Gates said. He was a bony, pop-eyed shrimp with uncombed hair and a nose bent like a macaw's.

"How're things?" Allen asked, as he plodded after the gaunt shape toward the neck of the underground shelter. Built during the war, the shelter was still intact. Gates and Sugermann had reinforced and improved it, Gates pounding nails and Sugermann overseeing.

"I was expecting Sugie. It's almost dawn on this side; he's been out all night buying supplies." Gates giggled, a nervous high-pitched twitter. "Trading big. We got a good hand, these days. Plenty of stuff people want; don't kid yourself."

The stairs brought them down to the shelter's main room. It was a litter of books, furniture, paintings, cans and boxes and jars of food, carpets and bric-a-brac and just plain junk. The phonograph was blaring a Chicago version of "I Can't Get Started." Gates turned it down, grinning.

"Make yourself at home." He tossed a box of crackers to Allen, and then a wedge of cheddar cheese. "Not hot — perfectly safe. Man, we've been digging, digging. Under all this ash, way down. Gates and Sugermann, archeologists for hire."

Remnants of the old. Tons of usable, partly usable, and ruined debris, objects of priceless worth, trinkets, indiscriminate trash. Allen seated himself on a carton of glassware. Vases and cups and tumblers and cut crystal.

"Pack rats," he said, examining a chipped bowl designed by some long-dead craftsman of the twentieth century. On the bowl was a design: a faun and hunter. "Not bad."

"Sell it to you," Gates offered. "Five bucks."

"Too much."

"Three bucks, then. We've got to move this stuff. Fast turnover, assure profit." Gates giggled happily. "What do you want? Bottle of Beringer's chablis? One thousand dollars. Copy of *The Decameron*? Two thousand dollars. Electric waffle iron?" He computed. "Depends on if you want the kind becomes a sandwich grill. That's more."

"Nothing for me," Allen murmured. Before him was a huge pile of moldering newspapers, magazines, books, tied with brown cord. *Saturday Evening Post*, the top one read.

"Six years of the *Post*," Gates said. "From 1947 to 1952. Lovely condition. Say, fifteen bills." He pawed into an opened stack beside the *Posts*, ripping and shredding violently. "Here's a sweet item. *Yale Review*. One of those 'little' magazines. Got stuff on Truman Capote, James Joyce." His eyes sparkled slyly. "Plenty of sex."

Allen examined a faded, water-logged book. It was cheaply bound, a bulging pulp with stained pages.

THE INDEFATIGABLE VIRGIN
Jack Woodsby

Opening at random he came across an absorbing paragraph.

" ... Her breasts were like two cones of white marble bulging within the torn covering of her thin silk dress. As he pulled her against him he could feel the hot panting need of her wonderful body. Her eyes were half-shut and she was moaning faintly. 'Please,' she gasped, trying feebly to push him away. Her dress slipped entirely aside, revealing the pulsing fullness of her taut, firm flesh . . .'"

"Good grief," Allen said.

"Fine book," Gates remarked, squatting down beside him. "Lots more. Here." He dug out another and pushed it at Allen. "Read."

I, THE KILLER

The author's name was blurred by time and decay. Opening the tattered paper-covered book, Allen read:

" . . . Again I shot her in the groin. Guts and blood spilled out, soaking through her torn skirt. The floor under my shoes was slippery with her gore. I accidently crushed one of her mangled breasts under my heel, but what the hell, she was dead . . ."

Bending down, Allen pulled out a fat, mildewed, gray-bound book and opened it.

" . . . Stephen Dedalus watched through the webbed window the lapidary's fingers prove a time-dulled chain. Dust webbed the window and the showtrays. Dust darkened the toiling fingers with their vulture nails . . ."

"That's a hot one," Gates said, peering over his shoulder. "Go on, look through it. At the end especially."

"Why is this here?" Allen asked.

Gates clapped his hands together and writhed. "Man, that's *the* one. That's the spiciest of them all. You know how much I get for a copy of that? Ten thousand dollars!" He tried to grab the book, but Allen hung onto it.

"... Dust slept on dull coils of bronze and silver, lozenges of cinnabar, on rubies, leprous and wine-dark stones ..."

Allen put down the book. "That's not bad." It gave him a queer feeling, and he reread the passage carefully.

There was a scraping at the stairs and Sugermann entered. "What's not bad?" He saw the book and nodded. "James Joyce. Excellent writer. *Ulysses* brings us a good deal, these days. More than Joyce himself ever got." He tossed down his armload. "Tom, there's a shipload up on the surface. Don't let me forget. We can get it down later." He, a heavy-set, round-faced man, with a stubble of bluish beard, began peeling off his wool overcoat.

Examining the copy of *Ulysses*, Allen said: "Why is this book with the others? It's entirely different."

"Has the same words," Sugermann said. He lit a cigarette and stuck it in a carved, ornate ivory holder. "How are you these days, Mr. Purcell? How's the Agency?"

"Fine," he said. The book bothered him. "But this—"

"This book is still pornography," Sugermann said. "Joyce, Hemingway. Degenerate trash. The Major's first Book Committee listed *Ulysses* on the hex-sheet back in 1988. Here." Laboriously, he scooped up a handful of books; first one and then another was tossed into Allen's lap. "A bunch more of them. Novels of the twentieth century. All gone, now. Banned. Burned. Destroyed."

"But what was the purpose of these books? Why are they lumped with the junk? They weren't once, were they?"

Sugermann was amused, and Gates cackled and slapped his knee.

"What kind of Morec did they teach?" Allen demanded.

"They didn't," Sugermann said. "These particular novels even taught *un*Morec."

"You've read these?" Allen scanned the volume of *Ulysses*. His interest and bewilderment grew. "Why? What did you find?"

Sugermann considered. "These, as discriminated from the others, are real books."

"What's that mean?"

"Hard to say. They're about something." A smile spread across Sugermann's face. "I'm an egghead, Purcell. I'd tell you these books are literature. So better not ask me."

"These guys," Gates explained, breathing into Allen's face, "wrote it all down, the way it was back in the Age of Waste." He hammered a book with his fist. "This tells. Everything's here."

"But these ought to be preserved," Allen said. "They shouldn't be tossed in with the trash. We need them as historical records."

"Certainly," Sugermann said. "So we'll know what life was like, then."

"They're valuable."

"Very valuable."

Angrily, Allen said: "They tell the truth!"

Sugermann bellowed with laughter. He got out a pocket handkerchief and wiped his eyes. "That's so, Purcell. They tell the truth, the one and only absolute truth." Suddenly he stopped laughing. "Tom, give him the Joyce book. As a present from you and me."

Gates was appalled. "But *Ulysses* is worth a hundred bills!"

"Give it to him." Sugermann sank into a growling, acrid stupor. "He should have it."

Allen said: "I can't take it; it's worth too much." And, he realized, he couldn't pay for it. He didn't have ten thousand dollars. And, he also realized, he wanted the book.

Sugermann glared at him for a long, disconcerting time. "Morec," he muttered at last. "No gift-giving. Okay, Allen. I'm sorry." He roused himself and went into the next room. "How about a glass of sherry?"

"That's good stuff," Gates said. "From Spain. The real thing."

Re-emerging with the half-empty bottle, Sugermann found three glasses and filled them. "Drink up, Purcell. To Goodness, Truth, and —" He considered. "Morality."

They drank.

Malparto made a final note and then signaled his technicians. The office lights came on as the trellis was wheeled away.

On the table the patient blinked, stirred, moved feebly.

"And then you came back?" Malparto asked.

"Yes," Mr. Coates said. "I drank three glasses of sherry and then I flew back to Newer York."

"And nothing else happened?"

Mr. Coates, with an effort, sat up. "I came back, parked the sliver, got the tools and bucket of red paint, and japed the statue. I left the empty paint can on a bench and walked home."

The first session was over and Malparto had learned absolutely nothing. Nothing had happened to his patient either before or at Hokkaido; he had met some boys, tried to buy a fifth of Scotch, had seen a book. That was all. It was senseless.

"Have you ever been Psi-tested?" Malparto asked.

"No." His patient squinted with pain. "Those drugs of yours gave me a headache."

"I have a few routine tests I'd like to give you. Perhaps next time; it's a trifle late, today." He had decided to cease the recall-therapy. There was no value in bringing to the surface past incidents and forgotten experiences. From now on he would work with the mind of Mr. Coates, not with its contents.

"Learn anything?" Mr. Coates asked, rising stiffly to his feet.

"A few things. One question. I'm curious to know the effect of this japery. In your opinion —"

"It gets me into trouble."

"I don't mean on you. I mean on the Morec Society."

Mr. Coates considered. "None. Except that it gives the police something to do. And the newspapers have something to print."

"How about the people who see the japed statue?"

"Nobody sees it; they've got it boarded up." Mr. Coates rubbed his jaw. "Your sister saw it. And some of the Cohorts saw it; they were rounded up to guard it."

Malparto made a note of that.

"Gretchen said that some of the Cohorts laughed. It was japed in an odd way; I suppose you've heard."

"I've heard," Malparto said. Later, he could get the facts from his sister. "So they laughed. Interesting."

"Why?"

"Well, the Cohorts are the storm-troopers of the Morec Society. They go out and do the dirty work. They're the teeth, the vigilantes. And they don't usually laugh."

At the office door Mr. Coates had paused. "I don't see the point."

Doctor Malparto was thinking: *precognition*. The ability to anticipate the future. "I'll see you Monday," he said, getting out his appointment book. "At nine. Will that be satisfactory?"

Mr. Coates said that it was satisfactory, and then he set off glumly for work.

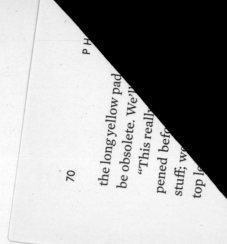

As he entered his office at the Agency, Doris appeared and said: "Mr. Purcell, something has happened. Harry Priar wants to tell you." Priar, who headed the Agency's art department, was his pro-term assistant, taking Fred Luddy's place.

Priar materialized, looking somber. "It's about Luddy."

"Isn't he gone?" Allen said, removing his coat. Malparto's drugs still affected him; his head ached and he felt dulled.

"He's gone," Priar said. "Gone to Blake-Moffet. We got a tip from T-M this morning, before you showed up."

Allen groaned.

"He knows everything we've got on tap," Priar continued. "All the new packets, all the current ideas. That means Blake-Moffet has them."

"Make an inventory," Allen said. "See what he took." He settled drearily down at his desk. "Let me know as soon as you're finished."

A whole day was consumed by inventory-taking. At five the information was in and on his desk.

"Picked us clean," Priar said. He admiringly shook his head. "Must have spent hours. Of course we can attach the material, try to get it back through the claims court."

"Blake-Moffet will fight for years," Allen said, fooling with

"By the time we get the packets back they'll have to dream up new ones. Better ones."

tough is," Priar said. "Nothing like this ever hap- re. We've had Blake-Moffet pirate stuff; we've lost 've been beaten to ideas. But we never had anybody at vel go over bag and baggage."

"We never fired anybody before," Allen reminded him. He was thinking how much Luddy resented the firing. "They can do us real harm. And with Luddy there they probably will. Grudge stuff. We've never run into that before. The personal element. Bitter, to-the-death tangling."

After Priar left, Allen got up and paced around his office. Tomorrow was Friday, his last full day to decide about the directorship of T-M. The statue problem would still be with him the rest of the week; as Malparto said, therapy would drag on indefinitely.

Either he went into T-M as he was now or he declined the job. On Saturday he would still be the same elusive personality, with the same switches to be pulled from deep within.

It was depressing to consider how little practical help the Health Resort had given him. Doctor Malparto was off in the clouds, thinking in terms of a lifetime of test-giving, reaction-measuring. And meanwhile the practical situation floundered. He had to make a decision, and without Malparto's help. Without, in effect, anybody's help. He was back where he started before Gretchen gave him the folded slip.

Picking up the phone he called his apartment.

"Hello," Janet's voice came, laden with dread.

"This is the Mortuary League," Allen said. "It is my duty to inform you that your husband was sucked into the manifold of an autofac ship and never heard from again." He examined his watch. "At precisely five-fifteen."

A terrible hushed silence, and then Janet said: "But that's *now*."

"If you listen," Allen said, "you can hear him breathing. He's not gone yet, but he's pretty far down."

Janet said: "You inhuman monster."

"What I want to find out," Allen said, "is what are we doing this evening?"

"I'm taking Lena's kids to the history museum." Lena was his wife's married sister. "You're not doing anything."

"I'll tag along," he decided. "I want to discuss something with you."

"Discuss what?" she asked instantly.

"Same old thing." The history museum would make as good a place as any; so many people passed through that no juvenile would single them out. "I'll be home around six. What's for dinner?"

"How about 'steak'?"

"Fine," he said, and hung up.

After dinner they walked over to Lena's and picked up the two kids. Ned was eight and Pat was seven, and they scurried excitedly along the twilight lane and up the steps of the museum. Allen and his wife came more slowly, hand in hand, saying little. For once the evening was pleasant. The sky was cloud-scattered but mild, and many people were out to enjoy themselves in the few ways open to them.

"Museums," Allen said. "And art exhibits. And concerts. And lectures. And discussions of public affairs." He thought of Gates' phonograph playing "I Can't Get Started," the taste of sherry, and, beyond everything else, the litter of the twentieth century that had focalized in the water-soaked copy of *Ulysses*. "And there's always Juggle."

Clinging wistfully to him, Janet said: "Sometimes I wish I was a kid again. Look at them go." The children had vanished inside the museum. To them the exhibits were still interesting; they hadn't wearied of the intricate tableaux.

"Someday," Allen said, "I'd like to take you where you can relax." He wondered where that would be. Certainly no place in the Morec scheme. Perhaps on some remote colony planet, when they had grown old and been discarded. "Your childhood days again. Where you can take off your shoes and wriggle your toes." As he had first found her: a shy, thin, very pretty girl, living with her nonleased family on bucolic Betelgeuse 4.

"Could we sometime take a trip?" Janet asked. "Anywhere — maybe to a place where there's open country and streams and—" She broke off. "And grass."

The hub of the museum was its twentieth century exhibit. An entire white-stucco house had been painstakingly reconstructed, with sidewalk and lawn, garage and parked Ford. The house was complete with furniture, robot mannequins, hot food on the table, scented water in the tile bathtub. It walked, talked, sang and glowed. The exhibit revolved in such a way that every part of the interior was visible. Visitors lined up at the circular railing and watched as Life in the Age of Waste rotated by.

Over the house was an illuminated sign:

HOW THEY LIVED

"Can I press the button?" Ned yammered, racing up to Allen. "Let me press it; nobody's pressed it. It's time to press it."

"Sure," Allen said. "Go ahead. Before somebody beats you to it."

Ned scampered back, squeezed to the railing where Pat waited, and jabbed the button. The spectators gazed benignly at the lush house and furnishings, knowing what was coming. They were watching, for a while, at least, the last of the house.

They drank in the opulence: the stocks of canned food, the great freezer and stove and sink and washer and drier, the car that seemed made of diamonds and emeralds.

Over the exhibit the sign winked out. An ugly cloud of smoke rolled up, obscuring the house. Its lights dimmed, turned dull red, and dried up. The exhibit trembled, and, to the spectators, a rumble came, the lazy tremor of a subterranean wind.

When the smoke departed, the house was gone. All that remained of the exhibit was an expanse of broken bones. A few steel supports jutted, and bricks and sections of stucco lay strewn everywhere.

In the ruins of the cellar the surviving mannikins huddled over their pitiful possessions: a tank of decontaminated water, a dog they were stewing, a radio, medicines. Only three mannikins had survived, and they were haggard and ill. Their clothing was in shreds and their skins were seared with radiation burns.

Over this hemisphere of the exhibit the sign concluded:

AND DIED

"Gee," Ned said, returning. "How do they do that?"

"Simple," Allen said. "The house isn't really in there, on that stage. It's an image projected from above. They merely substitute the alternate image. When you press the button it starts the cycle."

"Can I press it again?" Ned begged. "Please, I want to press it again; I want to blow the house up again."

As they wandered on, Allen said to his wife: "I wanted you to enjoy dinner. Have you?"

She clutched his arm. "Tell me."

"The whirlwind is coming back to be reaped. And it's an angry whirlwind. Luddy took off with everything he could lay his hands on, right to Blake-Moffet. He's probably vice president, with what he brought."

She nodded forlornly. "Oh."

"In a way, we're ruined. We have no backlog; all we are is a bunch of clever new ideas. And Luddy took them . . . roughly, us for the next year. That's how far ahead we had it. But that isn't the real problem. As an official of Blake-Moffet he'll be in a position to get back at me. And he will. Let's face it; I showed Luddy up for a sycophant. And that fun isn't."

"What are you going to do?"

"Defend myself, naturally. Luddy was a hard worker, competent, with a good sense of organization. But he wasn't original. He could take somebody else's idea — my idea — and milk a great deal from it. He used to build up whole packets from the smallest grain. But I have him on the creativity. So I can still run rings around Blake-Moffet, assuming I'm in the field a year from now."

"You sound almost — cheerful."

"Why not?" He shrugged. "It merely makes a bad situation worse. Blake-Moffet have always been the inertial stone dragging us into the grave. Every time they project a boy-gets-good-girl packet they blow the breath of age on us. We have to struggle out from under the dust before we can move." He pointed. "Like that house."

The opulent twentieth century house, with its Ford and Bendix washer, had reappeared. The cycle had returned to its source.

"How they lived," Allen quoted. "And died. That could be us. We're living now, but that doesn't mean anything."

"What happened at the Resort?"

"Nothing. I saw the Analyst; I recalled; I got up and left. Next Monday I go back."

"Can they help you?"

"Sure, given time."

Janet asked: "What are you going to do?"

"Take the job. Go to work as Director of Telemedia."

"I see." Then she asked: "Why?"

"Several reasons. First, because I can do a good job."

"What about the statue?"

"The statue isn't going away. Someday I'll find out why I japed it, but not by Saturday morning. Meanwhile, I'll have to live. And make decisions. By the way . . . the salary's about what I'm making now."

"If you're at T-M can Luddy hurt you more?"

"He can hurt the Agency more, because I'll be gone." He reflected. "Maybe I'll dismember it. I'll wait and see; it depends on how I do at T-M. In six months I may want to go back."

"What about you?"

Truthfully, he said: "He can hurt me more, too. I'll be fair game for everybody. Look at Mavis. Four giants in the field, and all of them trying to get into T-M. And I'll have one giant with a gnat stinging it."

"I suppose," Janet said, "that's another of the several reasons. You want to tangle with Luddy head-on."

"I want to meet him, yes. And I wouldn't mind hitting up against Blake-Moffet from that position. They're moribund; they're calcified. As Director of Telemedia I'll do my best to put them out of business."

"They probably expect that."

"Of course they do. One of their packets is enough for a year; I told Mrs. Frost that. As a competitor of Blake-Moffet I could run alongside them for years, hitting them now and then, getting hit in return. But as Director of T-M we'll have a grandiose showdown. Once I'm in, there's no other way."

Janet studied an exhibit of extinct flowers: poppies and lilies and gladioli and roses. "When are you going to tell Mrs. Frost?"

"I'll go over to her office tomorrow. She'll probably be expecting me . . . it's the last working day. Apparently she agrees with me on Blake-Moffet; this should please her. But that's another thing only time will tell."

The next morning he rented a little Getabout from a dealer and drove from his housing unit to the Committee building.

Myron Mavis, he reflected, would be giving up his within-walking-distance apartment. Protocol required that a man lease close to his job; in the next week or so it behooved him to ask for Mavis' setup. As Director of T-M he would need to live the role. There was slight latitude, and he was already resigned to the strictures. It was the price paid for public service in the higher brackets.

As soon as he entered the Committee building, the front secretary passed him through. There was no waiting, and, within five minutes, he was being ushered into Mrs. Frost's private office.

She rose graciously. "Mr. Purcell. How nice."

"You're looking well." They shook hands. "Is this a good time to talk to you?"

"Excellent," Mrs. Frost said, smiling. Today she wore a trim brown suit of some crisp fabric, unknown to him. "Sit down."

"Thank you." He seated himself facing her. "I see no point in waiting until the last moment."

"You've decided?"

Allen said: "I'll accept the job. And I apologize for stringing it out."

Waving her hand, Mrs. Frost dismissed his apology. "You should have time." And then her face glowed in a swift, beaming warmth of delight. "I'm so glad."

Touched, he said: "So am I." And he really meant it.

"When will you be ready to start?" She laughed and held up her hands. "Look at me; I'm as nervous as you."

"I want to start as soon as possible." He consulted with

himself; it would take at least a week to wind up affairs at the Agency. "What about a week from Monday?"

She was disappointed, but she suppressed it. "Yes, you should have that much time for the transfer. And — perhaps we can get together socially. For dinner some evening. And for Juggle. I'm quite a demon; I play every chance I get. And I'd like very much to meet your wife."

"Fine," Allen said, sharing her enthusiasm. "We'll arrange that."

11

THE DREAM, LARGE and gray, hanging like the tatters of a web, gathered itself around him and hugged him greedily. He screamed, but instead of sounds there drifted out of him stars. The stars rose until they reached the panoply of web, and there they struck fast, and were extinguished.

He screamed again, and this time the force of his voice rolled him downhill. Crashing through dripping vines he came to rest in a muddy trough, a furrow half-clogged with water. The water, brackish, stung his nostrils, choking him. He gasped, floundered, crept against roots.

It was a moist jungle of growing things in which he lay. The steaming hulks of plants pressed and shoved for water. They drank noisily, grew and expanded, split with a showering burst of particles. Around him the jungle altered through centuries of life. Moonlight, strained through bulging leaves, drizzled gummy and yellow around him, as thick as syrup.

And, in the midst of the creeping plant-pulp, was an artificial structure.

Toward it he struggled, reaching. The structure was flat, thin, with a brittle hardness. It was opaque. It was made of boards.

Joy submerged him as he touched its side. He screamed, and

this time the sound carried his body upward. He floated, drifted, clutched at the wood surface. His nails scrabbled, and splinters pierced his flesh. With a metal wheel he sawed through the wood and stripped it away, husk-like, dropping it and stamping on it. The wood broke loudly, echoing in the dream-silence.

Behind the wood was stone.

Gazing at the stone he felt awe. It had endured; it had not been carried away or destroyed. The stone loomed as he remembered it. No change had occurred, and that was very good. He felt the emotion all through him.

He reached out, and, bracing himself, plucked from the stone a round part of itself. Weighed down, he staggered off, and plunged head-first into the oozing warmth of plant-pulp.

For a time he lay gasping, his face pressed against slime. Once, an insect walked across his cheek. Far off, something stirred mournfully. At last, with great effort, he roused himself and began searching. The round stone lay half-buried in silt, at the edge of water. He found the metal wheel and cut away the groping roots. Then, bracing his knees, he lifted the stone and dragged it away, across a grassy hill so vast that it faded into infinity.

At the end of the hill he dropped the stone crashing into a little parked Getabout. Nobody saw him. It was almost dawn. The sky, streaked with yellow, would soon be drained, would soon become a hazy gray through which the sun could beat.

Getting into the front seat, he started up the steam pressure and drove carefully up the lane. The lane stretched out ahead of him, faintly damp, faintly luminous. On both sides housing units were jutting lumps of coal: oddly hardened organic substances. No light showed within them and nothing stirred.

When he reached his own housing unit he parked the car — making no sound — and began lugging the stone up the rear ramp. It took a long time, and he was trembling and perspiring when he reached his own floor. And still nobody saw him. He unlocked his door and dragged the stone inside.

Unhinged with relief, he sank down on the edge of the bed. It was over: he had done it. In her bed his wife stirred fretfully, sighed, turned over on her face. Janet did not wake up; nobody woke up. The city, the society, slept.

Presently he removed his clothes and climbed into bed. He fell asleep almost at once, his mind and body free of all tension, every trouble.

Dreamless, like an amoeba, he, too, slept.

12

SUNLIGHT STREAMED THROUGH the bedroom, warm and pleasant. Beside Allen in the bed lay his wife, also warm and pleasant. Her hair had tumbled against his face and now he turned to kiss her.

"Uh," Janet murmured, blinking.

"It's morning. Time to get up." But he, himself, remained inert. He felt lazy. Contentment spread through him; instead of getting up he put his arm around Janet and hugged her.

"Did the — tape go off?" she asked drowsily.

"This is Saturday. We're in charge, today." Caressing Janet's shoulder he said: "The pulsing fullness of firm flesh."

"Thank you," she murmured, yawning and stretching. Then she became serious. "Allen, were you sick last night?" Sitting up quickly, she said: "Around three o'clock you got out of bed and went to the bathroom. You were gone a long time."

"How long?" He had no memory of it.

"I fell asleep. So I can't say. But a long time."

In any case he felt fine, now. "You're thinking of earlier this week. You've got everything confused."

"No, it was last night. Early this morning." Wide-awake, she slid from the bed and onto her feet. "You didn't go out, did you?"

He thought about it. There was some vague phantasmagoria

in his mind, a confusion of dreamlike events. The taste of brackish water, the wet presence of plants. "I was on a distant jungle planet," he decided. "With torrid jungle priestesses whose breasts were like two cones of white marble." He tried to recall how the passage had read. "Bulging within the flimsy covering of her dress. Peeking through. Panting with hot need."

Exasperated, she caught hold of his arm and tugged. "Get up. I'm ashamed of you. You — adolescent."

Allen got to his feet and began searching for his towel. His arms, he discovered, were stiff. He flexed and unflexed his muscles, rubbed his wrists, inspected a scratch.

"Did you cut yourself?" Janet asked, alarmed.

He had. And, he noticed, the suit he had left on a hanger the night before now lay in a chaotic tumble on the floor. Lifting it up he spread it out on the bed and smoothed it. The suit was muddy and one trouser leg was torn.

Outside in the hall, doors opened and tenants wandered out to form the bathroom line. Sleepy voices muttered.

"Shall I go first?" Janet asked.

Still examining his suit he nodded. "Go ahead."

"Thank you." She opened the closet and reached for a slip and dress. "You're always so sweet to let me —" Her voice trailed off.

"What is it?"

"Allen!"

He bounded to the closet and lifted her aside.

On the floor of the closet was a bronzed thermoplastic head. The head stared nobly past him at a fixed point beyond. The head was huge, larger than life, a great solemn Dutch gargoyle head resting between pairs of shoes and the laundry bag. It was the head of Major Streiter.

"Oh God," Janet whispered, her hands to her face.

"Take it easy." He had never heard her blaspheme, and it added the final stamp of menace and collapse. "Go make sure the door's locked."

"It is." She returned. "That's part of the statue, isn't it?" Her voice shrilled. "Last night—*you went and got it*. That's where you were."

The jungle hadn't been a dream. He had stumbled through the dark, deserted Park, falling among the flowers and grass. Getting up and going on until he came to the boarded-up statue.

"How—did you get it home?" she asked.

"In the Getabout." The same Getabout, ironically, that he had rented to visit Sue Frost.

"What'll we do?" Janet said monotonously, her face stricken, caved in by the calamity. "Allen, what'll happen?"

"You get dressed and go wash." He began stripping off his pajamas. "And don't speak to anybody. Not one damn word."

She gave a muffled yip, then turned, caught up her robe and towel, and left. Alone, Allen selected an undamaged suit and dressed. By the time he was tying his necktie he had remembered the night's sequence pretty much intact.

"Then it's going to go on," Janet said, returning.

"Lock the door."

"You're still doing it." Her voice was thick, suppressed. In the bathroom she had swallowed a handful of sedatives and anti-anxiety pills. "It's not over."

"No," he admitted. "Apparently it's not."

"What comes next?"

"Don't ask me. I'm as mystified as you."

"You'll have to get rid of it." She came toward him accusingly. "You can't leave it lying around like part of a—corpse."

"It's safe enough." Presumably no one had seen him. Or, as before, he would already have been arrested.

"And you took that job. You're this way, doing insane things like this, and you accepted that job. You weren't drunk last night, were you?"

"No."

"So that isn't it. What is it, then?"

"Ask Doctor Malparto." He went to the phone and picked up the receiver. "Or maybe I will. If he's there." He dialed.

"Mental Health Resort," the friendly, bureaucratic voice answered.

"Is Doctor Malparto there today? This is a patient of his."

"Doctor Malparto will be in at eight. Shall I have him call you? Who is calling, please?"

"This is Mr. — Coates," Allen said. "Tell Doctor Malparto I'd like an emergency appointment. Tell him I'll be in at eight. I'll wait there until he can see me."

In his office at the Mental Health Resort, Doctor Malparto said with agitation: "What do you suppose happened?"

"Let him in and ask him." Gretchen stood by the window drinking a cup of coffee. "Don't keep him out there in the lounge; he's pacing like an animal. You're both so —"

"I don't have all my testing apparatus. Some of it's loaned to Heely's staff."

"He probably set fire to the Committee building."

"Don't be funny!"

"Maybe he did. Ask him; I'm curious."

"That night you bumped into him at the statue." He eyed his sister hostilely. "Did you know he had japed the statue?"

"I knew somebody had. No, I didn't know — what's the name you give him here?" She snatched up the dossier and leafed through it. "I was unaware that *Mr. Coates* was the japer. I went because I was interested. Nothing like that ever happened before."

"Boring world, isn't it?" Malparto strode down the corridor to the lounge and opened the door. "Mr. Coates, you may come in now."

Mr. Coates followed him rapidly. His face was strained and set, and he glared straight ahead. "I'm glad you could see me."

"You told the receptionist that it's urgent." Malparto ushered him into his office. "This is my sister, Gretchen. But you've already met."

"Hello," Gretchen said, sipping her coffee. "What have you done this time?"

Malparto saw his patient flinch.

"Sit down," Malparto said, showing him to a chair. Mr. Coates went obediently, and Malparto seated himself facing him. Gretchen remained at the window with her coffee cup. She obviously intended to stay.

"Coffee?" she asked, to Malparto's annoyance. "Black and hot. Real coffee, too. From vacuum tins, an old U.S. Army supply depot. Here." She filled a cup and passed it to Mr. Coates, who accepted it. "Almost the last."

"Very good," Mr. Coates murmured.

"Now," Malparto said, "I don't as a rule hold sessions this early. But in view of your extreme —"

"I stole the statue's head," Mr. Coates interrupted. "Last night, about three A.M."

Extraordinary, Malparto thought.

"I took it home, hid it in the closet. This morning Janet found it. And I called you."

"Do you —" Malparto hesitated, "have any plans for it?"

"None that I'm aware of."

Gretchen said: "I wonder what the market value would be."

"To help you," Malparto said, glancing irritably at his sister, "I must first gather information about your mind; I must learn its potentialities. Therefore I ask you to submit to a series of tests, the purpose of which is to determine your various psychic capacities."

His patient looked dubious. "Is that necessary?"

"The cause of your complex may lie outside the ordinary human range. It's my personal belief that you contain a unique psychological element." He dimmed the office lights. "You're familiar with the ESP deck?"

Mr. Coates made a faint motion.

"I am going to examine five cards," Malparto said. "You will not see their faces, only the backs. As I study them one by one I want you to tell me what each is. Are you ready to start?"

Mr. Coates made an even fainter motion.

"Good." Malparto drew a star card. He concentrated. "Do you receive an impression?"

Mr. Coates said: "Circle."

That was wrong, and Malparto went onto the next. "What is this one?"

"Square."

The telepathy test was a failure, and Malparto indicated so on his check-sheet. "Now," he stated, "we'll try a different test. This will not involve the reading of my mind." He shuffled the deck and laid five cards face-down on the desk. "Study their backs and tell me each one in order."

His patient got one out of the five.

"We'll leave the deck for a moment." Malparto brought out the dice-rolling cage and set it into motion. "Observe these dice. They fall in a random pattern. I want you to concentrate on a particular showing: seven, or five, anything that can come up."

His patient concentrated on the dice for fifteen minutes. At the end of that time Malparto compared the showing with the statistical tables. No significant change could be observed.

"Back to the cards," Malparto said, gathering up the deck.

"We'll give you a test for precognition. In this test I'll ask you what card I'm *about* to select." He laid the deck down and waited.

"Circle," Mr. Coates said listlessly.

Malparto handed his sister the check-sheet, and he kept the precog test going for almost an hour. At the end of that time his patient was surly and exhausted, and the results were inconclusive.

"The cards don't lie," Gretchen quoted, handing back the sheet.

"What do you mean by that?"

"I mean go on to the next test."

"Mr. Coates," Malparto said, "do you feel able to continue?"

His patient blearily raised his head. "Is this getting us anywhere?"

"I think it is. It's clear that you don't possess any of the usual extra-sensory talents. It's my hunch that you're a Psi-plus. Your talent is of a less common nature."

"EEP," Gretchen said tartly. "*Extra* extra-sensory perception."

"The first of this series," Malparto said, ignoring her, "will involve the projection of your will on another human." He unfolded his blackboard and chalk stick. "As I stand here, you concentrate on forcing me to write certain numbers. It should be your will superimposed over mine."

Time passed. Finally, feeling a few vague tendrils of psychic will, Malparto wrote: 3–6–9.

"Wrong," Mr. Coates murmured. "I was thinking 7,842."

"Now," Malparto said, setting out a small gray stone, "I want you to duplicate this inorganic matter. Try to summon a replica immediately tangent to it."

That test was a failure, too. Disappointed, Malparto put the stone away.

"Now levitation. Mr. Coates, I want you to close your eyes and attempt — psychically — to lift yourself from the floor."

Mr. Coates attempted, without result.

"Next," Malparto said, "I want you to place your open palm against the wall behind you. Push, and at the same time, concentrate on passing your hand *between* the molecules of the wall."

The hand failed to pass between the molecules.

"This time," Malparto said gamely, "we'll attempt to measure your ability to communicate with lower life forms." A lizard, in a box, was brought out. "Stand with your head near the lid. See if you can tune into the lizard's mental pattern."

There was no result.

"Maybe the lizard has no mental pattern," Mr. Coates said.

"Nonsense." Malparto's annoyance was growing wildly. He brought forth a hair resting in a dish of water. "See if you can animate the hair. Try to transform it into a worm."

Mr. Coates failed.

"Were you really trying?" Gretchen asked.

Mr. Coates smiled. "Very hard."

"I should think that would be easy enough," she said. "There's not much difference between a hair and a worm. On a cloudy day —"

"Now," Malparto broke in, "we'll test your ability to heal." He had noticed the scratch on Allen's wrist. "Direct your psychic powers toward that damaged tissue. Try to restore it to health."

The scratch remained.

"Too bad," Gretchen said. "That would be a useful one."

Malparto, overcome by abandon, brought out a water wand and asked his patient to divine. A bowl of water was skillfully hidden, and Mr. Coates lumbered about the office. The wand did not dip.

"Bad wood," Gretchen said.

Depressed, Malparto examined the list of remaining tests:

Ability to contact spirits of the dead
Capacity to transmute lead into gold
Ability to assume alternate forms
Ability to create rain of vermin and/or filth
Power to kill or damage at a distance

"I have a feeling," he said finally, "that due to fatigue you're growing subconsciously uncooperative. Therefore it's my decision that we defer the balance of the tests to some other time."

Gretchen asked Mr. Coates: "Can you kindle fire? Can you slay seven with one blow? Can your father lick my father?"

"I can steal," the patient said.

"That's not much. Anything else?"

He reflected. "Afraid that's all." Getting to his feet he said to Malparto: "I assume the Monday appointment is void."

"You're leaving?"

"Well," he said, "there's no point sticking around here." He reached for the doorknob. "We haven't got anywhere."

"And you won't be coming back?"

At the door he paused. "Probably not," he decided. At the moment all he wanted to do was go home. "If I change my mind I'll call you." He started to pull the door shut.

That was when all the lights went out around him.

13

RUMBLE RUMBLE.

The bus lifted from the stop and continued across roof tops. Houses sparkled beneath, in planned patterns, separated by lawns. A swimming pool lay like a blue eye. But, he noticed, the pool far below was not perfectly round. At one end the tiles formed a patio. He saw tables, beach umbrellas. Tiny shapes were people reclining at leisure.

"Four," the bus said metallically.

A woman rose and found the rear door. The bus lowered to the stop, the door slithered aside, the woman stepped down.

"Watch your step," the bus said. "Exit by the rear." It ascended, and again houses sparkled beneath.

Next to Allen the large gentleman mopped his forehead. "Warm day."

"Yes," Allen agreed. To himself he said: *Say nothing. Do nothing. Don't even move.*

"You hold this a minute, young fellow? Like to tie my shoe." The large gentleman passed his armload of bundles across. "Go shopping you have to lug it home. That's the gimmick."

"Five," the bus said. Nobody got up, so the bus continued. Below, a shopping section was visible: a clump of bright stores.

"They say shop near home," the large gentleman said, "but

you can save money if you go downtown. Sales, you know. They buy in quantity." Out of a long paper bag he lifted a jacket. "Nice, eh? Real cow." He showed Allen a can of wax. "Got to keep it moist or it cracks. Rain's bad for it. Another gimmick. But you can't have everything."

"Exit by the rear," the bus said. "No smoking. Step to the back, please." More houses passed beneath.

"You feel all right?" the large gentleman asked. "Seems to me you look like you might have a touch of sunstroke. A lot of people, they go out in the sun on a hot day like this. Don't know any better." He chuckled. "Feel cold? Nauseated?"

"Yes," Allen said.

"Probably been running around playing Quart. You a pretty good quartist?" He sized Allen up. "Good shoulders, arms. Young fellow like you probably be right-wing. Eh?"

"Not yet," Allen said. He looked through the window of the bus and then down through the transparent floor at the city. Into his mind came the thought that he didn't even know where to get off. He didn't know where he was going or why or where he was now.

He was not in the Health Resort. That was the sole fact, and he took hold of it and made it the hub of his new universe. He made it the reference point and he began to creep cautiously from there.

This was not the Morec society, because there were no swimming pools and wide lawns and separate houses and glass-bottomed busses in the Morec society. There were no people basking in the sun in the middle of the day. There was no game called *Quart*. And this was not a vast historical exhibit such as the twentieth century house in the museum, because he could see the date on the magazine being read across the aisle, and it was the right month and year.

"Can I ask you something?" he said to the large gentleman.

"Surely." The large gentleman beamed.

"What's the name of this town?"

The large gentleman's face changed color. "Why, this is Chicago."

"Six," the bus said. Two young women got up, and the bus lowered to let them off. "Exit at the rear. No smoking, please."

Allen got up, squeezed to the aisle, and followed the women from the bus.

The air smelled fresh, full of the nearness of trees. He took a deep breath, walked a few steps, halted. The bus had let him off in a residential section; only houses were visible, set along wide, tree-lined streets. Children were playing, and, on the lawn of one house, a girl was sun-bathing. Here body was quite tan and her breasts were highly upraised. And her nipples were a pretty pastel pink.

If anything proved his separation from the Morec society it was the naked young lady stretched out on the grass. He had never seen anything like it. In spite of himself he walked that way.

"What are you looking at?" the girl asked, her head on her folded arms, face-up in the deep green lawn.

"I'm lost." It was the first thing that entered his mind.

"This is Holly Street and the cross street is Glen. Where do you want to be?"

"I want to be home," he said.

"Where's that?"

"I don't know."

"Look at your ident card. In your wallet."

He reached into his coat and brought out his wallet. The card was there, a strip of plastic with words and numbers punched into it.

2319 Pepper Lane

That was his address, and above it was his name. He read that, too.

Coates, John B.

"I slipped over," he said.

"Over what?" She raised her head.

Bending down he showed her the ident card. "Look, it says John Coates. But my name's Allen Purcell; I picked the name Coates at random." He ran his thumb across the raised plastic, feeling it.

The girl sat up and tucked her bare, deeply-tanned legs under her. Her breasts, even as she sat, remained up-tilted. Her nipples projected prettily. "Very interesting," she said.

"Now I'm Mr. Coates."

"Then what happened to Allen Purcell?" She smoothed her hair back and smiled up.

"He must be back there," Mr. Coates said. "But I'm Allen Purcell," Allen said. "It doesn't make sense."

Sliding to her feet the girl put a hand on his shoulder and guided him to the sidewalk. "On the corner is a cab-box. Ask the cab to take you home. Pepper Lane is about two miles from here. Do you want me to call it for you?"

"No," he said. "I can do it."

He set off along the pavement, looking for the cab-box. Never having seen one, he walked past it.

"There," the girl called, hands cupped to her mouth.

Nodding, he pulled the switch. A moment later the cab dropped to the pavement beside him and said: "Where to, sir?"

The trip took only a minute. The cab landed; he pushed coins into its slot; and then he was standing before a house.

His house.

The house was big, imposing, dominating a ridge of cedars and peppers. Sprinklers hurled water across the sloping lawns on both sides of the brick path. In the rear was a garden of dahlias and wisteria, a tumbling patch of deep red and purple.

On the front porch was a baby. An agile sitter perched on the railing nearby, its lens monitoring. The baby noticed Mr. Coates; smiling, it reached up its arm and burbled.

The front door — solid hard wood, with brass inlay — was wide open. From within the house drifted the sounds of music: a jazzy dance band.

He entered.

The living room was deserted. He examined the rug, the fireplace, the piano, and he recognized it from his research. Reaching, he plinked a few notes. Then he wandered into the dining room. A large mahogany table filled the center. On the table was a vase of iris. Along two walls were a line of mounted plates, glazed and ornate; he inspected them and then passed on, into a hall. Broad stairs led up: he gazed up, saw a landing and open doors, then turned toward the kitchen.

The kitchen overwhelmed him. It was long, gleaming-white, and it contained every kind of appliance he had heard of and some he had not. On the immense stove a meal was cooking, and he peered into a pot, sniffing. Lamb, he decided.

While he was sniffing there was a noise behind him. The back door opened and a woman entered, breathless and flushed.

"Darling!" she exclaimed, hurrying to him. "When did you get home?"

She was dark, with tumbles of hair bouncing against her shoulders. Her eyes were huge and intense. She wore shorts and a halter and sandals.

She was Gretchen Malparto.

The clock on the mantel read four-thirty. Gretchen had drawn the drapes, and the living room was in shadow. Now she paced about, smoking, gesturing jerkily. She had changed to a print skirt and peasant blouse. The baby, whom Gretchen called "Donna," was upstairs in her crib, asleep.

"Something's wrong," Gretchen repeated. "I wish you'd tell me what it is. Damn it, do I have to beg?" Turning, she faced him defiantly. "Johnny, this isn't like you."

He lay on the couch, stretched out, a gin sling in one hand. Above him the ceiling was a mild green, and he contemplated it until Gretchen's voice shattered at him.

"Johnny, for Christ's sake!"

He roused himself. "I'm right here. I'm not standing outdoors."

"Tell me what happened." She came over and settled on the arm of the couch. "Is it because of what happened Wednesday?"

"What happened Wednesday?" He was, in a detached way, interested.

"At Frank's party. When you found me upstairs with —" She looked away. "I forget his name. The tall, blond-haired one. You seemed mad; you were a little this way. Is that it? I thought we agreed not to interfere with each other. Or do you want it to work just one way?"

He asked: "How long have we been married?"

"This is a lecture, I suppose." She sighed. "Go ahead. Then it's my turn."

"Just answer my question."

"I forget."

Meditating, he said: "I thought wives always knew."

"Oh, come off it." She pulled away and stalked over to the phonograph. "Let's eat. I'll have it serve us. Or do you want to go out for dinner? Maybe you'll feel better where there's people — instead of cooped up here."

He didn't feel cooped up. From where he lay he could see most of the downstairs of the house. Room after room . . . like living in an office building. Renting a whole floor; two floors. And in the back of the house, in the garden, was a three-room guest cottage.

In fact, he felt nothing at all. The gin sling had anesthetized him.

"Care to buy a head?" he asked her.

"I don't understand."

"A stone head. Bronzed thermoplastic, to be absolutely accurate. Responds to cutting tools. Doesn't that ring a bell? You thought the job was quite original."

"Rave away."

He said: "A year? Two years? Approximately."

"We were married in April 2110. So it must be four years."

"That's a good long time," he said. "Mrs. Coates."

"Yes, Mr. Coates."

"And this house?" He liked the house.

"This house," Gretchen said fiercely, "belonged to your mother. And I'm sick of hearing about it. I wish we had never moved here; I wish we had sold the goddamn thing. We could have got a good price two years ago; now real estate's down."

"It'll go up. It always does."

Glaring at him, Gretchen strode across the living room to the hall. "I'll be upstairs, changing for dinner. Tell it to serve."

"Serve," he said.

With a snort of exasperation, Gretchen left. He heard the click of her heels on the stairs and then that, too, faded.

The house was lovely: it was spacious, luxuriously furnished, solidly built, and modern. It would last a century. The garden was full of flowers and the freezer was full of food. Like heaven, he thought. Like a vision of the after-reward, for all the years of public service. For all the sacrifice and struggle, bickerings and Mrs. Birmingham. The ordeal of the block meetings. The tension and sternness of the Morec society.

A part of him reached out to this, and he knew what that part was named. John Coates was now in his own world, and it was the antithesis of Morec.

Close to his ear, a voice said: "There remains some island of ego."

A second voice, a woman's, said: "But submerged."

"Totally withdrawn," the man said. "The shock of failure. When the Psi-testing collapsed. He was at the edge of the Resort, starting back out. And he couldn't."

The woman asked: "Isn't there a better solution?"

"He needed one at that instant. He couldn't return to Morec, and he had found no help at the Resort. For that I'm partly to blame; I wasted time on the testing."

"You thought it would help." The woman seemed to be moving nearer. "Can he hear us?"

"I doubt it. There's no way to tell. The catalepsy is complete, so he can't signal."

"How long will it last?"

"Hard to say. Days, weeks, maybe the balance of his life." Malparto's voice seemed to recede, and he strained to catch it. "Maybe we should inform his wife."

"Can you tell anything about his inner world?" Gretchen, too, was dimming. "What kind of fantasy is he lost in?"

"An escape." The voice vanished, then momentarily returned. "Time will tell." It was gone.

Struggling from the couch, Mr. John Coates shouted: "Did you hear them? *Did you?*"

At the top of the stairs Gretchen appeared, hairbrush in one hand, stockings over her arm. "What's the matter?"

He appealed in despair. "It was you and your brother. Couldn't you hear them? This is a —" He broke off.

"A what?" She came calmly downstairs. "What are you talking about?"

A pool had formed where his drink glass had fallen; he bent down to sop it up. "I have news for you," he said. "This is real. I'm sick; this is a psychotic retreat."

"I'm surprised at you," she said. "Really, I am. You sound like a college sophomore. Solipsism — skepticism. Bishop Berkeley, all that ultimate-reality stuff."

As his fingers touched the drink glass, the wall behind it vanished.

Still stooping, he saw out into the world beyond. He saw the street, other houses. He was afraid to lift his head. The mantel and fireplace, the rug and deep chairs . . . even the lamp and bric-a-brac, all were gone. Only a void. Emptiness.

"There it is," Gretchen said. "Right by your hand."

He saw no glass, not; it had vanished with the room. In spite of himself, he turned his head. There was nothing behind him. Gretchen was gone, too. He was standing alone in emptiness. Only the next house, a long way off, remained. Along the street a car moved, followed by a second. At a neighboring house a curtain was drawn. Darkness was descending everywhere.

"Gretchen," he said.

There was no response. Only silence.

14

HE CLOSED HIS eyes and willed. He imagined the room: he pictured Gretchen, the coffee table, the package of cigarettes, the lighter beside it. He pictured the ashtray, the drapes, the couch and phonograph.

When he opened his eyes the room was back. But Gretchen was gone. He was alone in the house.

The shades were all down, and he had a deep intuition of lateness. As if, he thought, time had passed. A clock on the mantel read eight-thirty. Had four whole hours gone by? Four hours . . .

"Gretchen?" he said, experimentally. He went to the stairs and started up. Still no sign of her. The house was warm, the air pleasant and fresh. Somewhere an automatic heating unit functioned.

A room to his right was her bedroom. He glanced in.

The small ivory clock on the dressing table did not read eight-thirty. It read a quarter to five. Gretchen had overlooked it. She had not set it forward with the one downstairs.

Instantly he was running back downstairs, two steps at a time.

The voices had reached him as he lay on the couch. Kneeling, he pressed his hands over the fabric, across the arms and back, under the cushions. Finally he dragged the couch away from the wall.

The first speaker was mounted within a coil of backspring. A second and then a third were concealed under the rug; they were as flat as paper. He estimated that at least a dozen speakers had been mounted throughout the room.

Since Gretchen had been upstairs the control unit was undoubtedly there. Again he climbed the stairs and entered her bedroom.

At first he failed to recognize it. The control lay in plain sight, on the woman's dressing table, with the jars and tubes and packages of cosmetics. The hairbrush. He picked it up and rotated the plastic handle.

From downstairs boomed a man's voice. "There remains some island of ego."

Gretchen's voice answered. "But submerged."

"Totally withdrawn," Malparto continued. "The shock—" The tape transport, mounted somewhere in the walls of the house, had halted in the middle of its cycle.

Downstairs again, he searched for the means by which Gretchen had dissolved the house. When he found it, he was chagrined. The unit was built into the fireplace, in open view, one of the many comfort-making gadgets. He pressed the stud and the room around him with its furnishings and rich textures seeped away. The outside world remained: houses, the street, the sky. A glimmer of stars.

The device was a mere romantic gadget. For long, dull evenings. Gretchen was an active girl.

In a closet, under a heap of blankets, he found a newspaper used as a shelf-liner; it was empirical proof. The newspaper was the Vega *Sentinel*. He was not in a fantasy world; he was on the fourth planet of the Vega System.

He was on the Other World, the permanent refuge maintained by the Mental Health Resort. Maintained for persons who had come — not for therapy — but for sanctuary.

Finding the phone, he dialed zero.

"Number please," the operator said, the faint, tinny, and terribly reassuring voice.

"Give me one of the space ports," he said. "Any one that has inter-system service."

A series of clicks, buzzes, and then he was connected with the ticket office. A methodical male voice on the other end of the wire said,

"Yes sir. What can I do for you?"

"What's the fare to Earth?" He wondered, in a stricken way, just how long he had been here. A week? A month?

"One way, first class. Nine hundred thirty dollars. Plus twenty percent luxury tax." The voice was without emotion.

He had no such money. "What's the next system in order?"

"Sirius."

"How much is that?" He didn't have over fifty dollars in his wallet. And this planet was under the jurisdiction of the Health Resort: it had acquired it with its deed.

"One way, first class. Tax included . . . comes to seven hundred forty-two dollars."

He calculated. "What's it cost to phone Earth?"

The ticket agent said, "You'll have to ask the phone company, mister. That's not our business."

When he had gotten the operator again, Allen said, "I'd like to place a call to Earth."

"Yes sir." She did not seem surprised. "What number, sir?"

He gave Telemedia's number, and then the number on the phone he was using. It was as simple as that.

After several minutes of buzzing, the operator said, "I'm sorry, sir. Your party does not answer."

"What time is it there?"

A moment and then: "In that time zone it is three A.M., sir."

In a husky voice he said, "Look, I've been kidnapped. I have to get out of here — back to Earth."

"I suggest you call one of the inter-system transport fields, sir," the operator said.

"All I've got is fifty bucks!"

"I'm sorry, sir. I can connect you with one of the fields if you wish."

He hung up.

There was no point staying in the house, but he lingered long enough to type out a note — a note with a vengeance. He left the note in the middle of the coffee table, where Gretchen would be sure to see it.

> Dear Mrs. Coates,
>
> You remember Molly. Damned if I didn't run into her at the Brass Poker. Says she's pregnant, but you know how that kind are. Think I better stay with her until we can get her a you-know-what. Expensive, but it's the price you pay.

He signed it *Johnny* and then left the house.

Other World had plenty of roving taxis, and within five minutes he was in the downtown business district with its lights and flow of people.

At the space port a full-size ship stood upright on its tail. He guessed, with almost frenzied despair, that it was in the process of leaving for the next system. A line of supply trucks dashed back and forth; the ship was already in the final stages of loading.

Paying off the taxi, he tramped across the gravel parking lot of the field, down the street until he arrived at a syndrome of life: a restaurant doing an active business, full of patrons and noise and chatter. Feeling like a fool he buttoned his coat up around him and strode through the doorway to the cashier.

"Put up your hands, lady," he said, jutting out his pocket. "Before I put a McAllister heat beam through your head."

The girl gasped, raised her hands, opened her mouth and gave a terrified bleat. Patrons at nearby tables glanced up in disbelief.

"Okay," Allen said, in a normally-loud voice. "Now let's have the money. Push it across the counter before I blow out your brains with my McAllister heat beam."

"Oh dear," the girl said.

From behind him two Other World police wearing helmets and crisp blue uniforms appeared and grabbed his arms. The girl flopped out of sight and Allen's hand was yanked from his pocket.

"A noose," one cop said. "A supernoose. It's troublemakers like this ruin a clean neighborhood."

"Let go of me," Allen said. "Before I blow off your heads with my McAllister heat beam."

"Buddy," one of the cops said, as they dragged him from the restaurant, "this cancels the Resort's obligations to succor you. You've shown your unreliability by committing a felony."

"I'll blow all of you to bits," Allen said, as they bundled him into the police car. "This heat beam talks."

"Get his ident." A cop snatched Allen's wallet. "John B. Coates. 2319 Pepper Lane. Well, Mr. Coates, you've had your chance. Now you're on your way back to Morec. How does that sound?"

"You won't live to send me back," Allen said. The car was sprinting toward the field, and the big ship was still there. "I'll get you. You'll see."

The car, flying a foot above the gravel, turned into the field and made directly for the ship. The siren came on; field attendants stopped work and watched.

"Tell them to hold it," one of the cops said. He got out a microphone and contacted the field's tower. "Another supernoose. Open up the fleebee."

In a matter of seconds the car had come alongside the ship, the doors had united, and Allen was in the hands of the ship's sheriff.

"Welcome back to Morec," a run-down fellow supernoose muttered, as Allen was deposited beside him in the restricted area.

"Thanks," Allen said, with relief. "It's good to be back." Now he was wondering if he would reach Earth by Sunday. On Monday morning his job at Telemedia started. Had he lost too much time?

Whoosh, the floor went. The ship was rising.

15

THE TRIP BEGAN Wednesday night, and by Sunday night he was back on Earth. The notation was arbitrary, of course, but the interval was real. Tired, sweaty, Allen emerged from the ship and back into the Morec society.

The field was not far from the Spire and his housing unit, but he balked at the idea of walking. It seemed unnecessarily strict; the supplicants in Other World showed no sign of degeneracy because they rode busses. Going into a phone booth at the field he called Janet.

"Oh!" she gasped. "They released you? You're — all right?"

He asked: "What did Malparto tell you?"

"They said you had gone to Other World for treatment. They said you might be there several weeks."

Now it made even more sense. In several weeks he would have lost his directorship and his status in the Morec world. After that it wouldn't matter if he discovered the hoax or not; without a lease, without a job, he would fairly well have to remain on Vega 4.

"Did he say anything about you joining me?"

There was a hasty flutter from the phone. "Y-yes, he did. He said you'd adjust to Other World, but if you couldn't adjust to this, then —"

"I didn't adjust to Other World. Just a lot of people lounging around sun-bathing. Is that Getabout still there? The one I rented?"

Janet, it developed, had returned the Getabout to the rental outfit. The charge was steep, and the Health Resort had already begun to tap his salary. Somehow that seemed to complete the outrage: the Resort, in the guise of helping him, had kidnapped him, and then billed him for services rendered.

"I'll get another." He started to hang up, then asked: "Has Mrs. Frost been around?"

"She phoned several times."

That sounded ominous. "What'd you tell her? That my mind gave out and I fled to the Resort?"

"I said you were winding up your affairs and couldn't be disturbed." Janet breathed huskily into the phone, deafening him. "Allen, I'm so glad you're back. I was so worried."

"How many pills did you swallow?"

"Well, quite a few. I — couldn't sleep."

He hung up, dug out another quarter, and dialed Sue Frost's personal number. After a time she answered . . . the familiar calm, dignified voice.

"This is Allen," he said. "Allen Purcell. I just wanted to check with you. Things coming along all right at your end?"

"Mr. Purcell," she said harshly, "be at my apartment in ten minutes. This an order is!"

Click.

He stared at the dead phone. Then he left the phone booth and started walking.

The Frost apartment directly overlooked the Spire, as did the apartments of all Committee Secretaries. Allen took a reassuring breath and then climbed the stairs. A clean shirt, a bath, and a long rest would have helped, but there was no time for luxuries. And he could, of course, pass his appearance off as the effects of a week or so spent closing down business; he had been slaving night and day at the Agency, trying to get all the loose ends to come out. With that in mind he rang Mrs. Frost's doorbell.

"Come in." She stood aside and he entered. In the single room sat Myron Mavis looking weary, and Ida Pease Hoyt looking grim and formal.

"Hello," Allen said, with a strong sense of doom.

"Now," Mrs. Frost said, coming around in front of him. "Where have you been? You weren't at your Agency; we checked there a number of times. We even sent a bonded representative to sit in with your staff. A Mr. Priar is operating Allen Purcell, Inc. during your absence."

Allen wondered if he should lie or tell the truth. He decided to lie. The Morec society couldn't bear the truth; it would punish him and keep on going. And somebody else would be named Director of T-M, a creature of Blake-Moffet.

"Harry Priar is acting administrator," he said. "As Myron here is acting Director of T-M until I take over. Are you trying to say I've been on salary the last week?" That certainly wasn't so. "The understanding was clear enough: I go to work next Monday, tomorrow. This past week has been my own. T-M has no more claim over me this past week than it had last year."

"The point—" Mrs. Frost began, and then the doorbell sounded. "Excuse me. This should be them now."

When the door opened Tony Blake from Blake-Moffet entered. Behind him was Fred Luddy, a briefcase under his arm. "Good evening, Sue," Tony Blake said agreeably. He was a portly, well-dressed man in his late fifties, with snow-white hair and rimless glasses. "Evening, Myron. This is an honor, Mrs. Hoyt. Evening, Allen. Glad to see you back."

Luddy said nothing. They all seated themselves, facing one

another, swapping tension and hauteur. Allen was acutely aware of his baggy suit and unstarched shirt; by the minute he looked less like an overworked businessman and more like a college radical from the Age of Waste.

"To continue," Mrs. Frost said. "Mr. Purcell, you were not at your Agency as your wife told us. At first we were puzzled, because we believed there was going to be mutual confidence between us. It seemed odd that a situation of this sort, with your dropping mysteriously out of sight, and these vague evasions and denials by your—"

"Now look here," Allen said. "You're not addressing a metazoon and a mammal; you're addressing a human being who's a citizen of the Morec society. Either you speak to me civilly or I leave now. I'm tired and I'd like to get some sleep. I'll leave it up to you."

Curtly, Mrs. Hoyt said: "He's quite right, Sue. Stop playing boss, and for heaven's sake get that righteous look off your face. Leave that to God."

"Perhaps you don't have confidence in me," Mrs. Frost answered, turning. "Should we settle that first?"

Sprawled out in his chair, Myron Mavis snickered. "Yes, I'd like this one better. Do settle it first, Sue."

Mrs. Frost became flustered. "Really, this whole thing is getting out of hand. Why don't I fix coffee?" She arose. "And there's a little brandy, if nobody feels it's contrary to public interest."

"We're sinking," Mavis said, grinning across at Allen. "Glub, glub. Under the waves of sin."

The tension ebbed and both Blake and Luddy began shuffling, conferring, murmuring. Luddy put on his horn-rimmed glasses and two serious heads were bent over the contents of his briefcase. Mrs. Frost went to the hotplate and put on the coffeemaker. Still seated, Mrs. Hoyt regarded a spot on the floor and spoke to no one. As always, she wore heavy furs, dark stockings, and low-heeled shoes. Allen had a great deal of respect for her; he knew her for an adroit manipulator.

"You're related to Major Streiter," he said. "Isn't that what I've heard?"

Mrs. Hoyt favored him with a look. "Yes, Mr. Purcell. The Major was a progenitor on my father's side."

"Terrible about the statue," Blake put in. "Imagine an outbreak like that. It defies description."

Allen had forgotten about the statue. And the head. It was still in the closet, unless Janet had done something with it. No wonder she had gulped down bottles of pills: the head had been there with her, all during the week.

"They'll catch him," Luddy said, with vigor. "Or them. Personally it's my conviction that an organized gang is involved."

"There's something almost satanic in it," Sue Frost said. "Stealing the head, that way. Coming back a few days later and — right in front of the police — stealing it and taking it heaven knows where. I wonder if it'll ever turn up." She located cups and saucers.

When the coffee had been served, the discussion took up where it had left off. But moderation prevailed. Cooler heads were at work.

"Certainly there's no reason to quarrel," Mrs. Frost said. "I suppose I was upset. Honestly, Allen, look at the spot you put us in. Last Sunday — a week ago — I picked up the phone and called your apartment; I wanted to catch you with your wife so we could decide on our Juggle evening."

"I'm sorry," Allen murmured, scrutinizing the wall and mentally twiddling his thumbs. In some ways this was the worst part, the rhetoric of apology.

"Would you like to tell us what happened?" Mrs. Frost continued. Her savior-faire had returned, and she smiled with her usual grace and charm. "Consider this a friendly inquiry. We're all your friends, even Mr. Luddy."

"What's the Blake-Moffet team doing here?" he asked. "I can't see how this concerns them. Maybe I'm being overly blunt, but this seems to be a matter between you and me and Mrs. Hoyt."

A pained exchange of glances informed him that there was more to it. As if the presence of Blake and Luddy hadn't said that already.

"Come on, Sue," Mrs. Hoyt rumbled in her gravelly voice.

"When we couldn't get in touch with you," Mrs. Frost went on, "we had a conference and we decided to sit on it. After all, you're a grown man. But then Mr. Blake called us. T-M has done a great deal of business with Blake-Moffet over the years, and we all know one another. Mr. Blake showed us some disturbing material, and we —"

"What material?" Allen demanded. "Let's have a look at it."

Blake answered. "It's here, Purcell. Don't get upset; all in due time." He tossed some papers over, and Allen caught them. While he examined them Mrs. Frost said:

"I'd like to ask you, Allen. As a personal friend. Never mind those papers; I'll tell you what it is. You haven't separated from your wife, have you? You haven't had a quarrel you'd rather keep quiet, something that's come up between you that means a more or less permanent altercation?"

"Is that what this is about?" He felt as if he had been dipped in sheer cold. It was one of those eternal blind alleys that Morec worriers got themselves into. Divorce, scandal, sex, other women — the whole confused gamut of marital difficulty.

"Naturally," Mrs. Hoyt said, "it would be incumbent on you to refuse the directorship under such circumstances. A man in such a high position of trust — well, you're familiar with the rest."

The papers in his hands danced in a jumble of words, phrases, dates and locations. He gave up and tossed them aside. "And Blake's got documentation on this?" They were after him, but they had got themselves onto a false lead. Luckily for him. "Let's hear it."

Blake cleared his throat and said: "Two weeks ago you worked alone at your Agency. At eight-thirty you locked up and left. You walked at random, entered a commissary, then returned to the Agency and took a ship."

"What then?" He wondered how far they had gone.

"Then you eluded pursuit. We, ah, weren't equipped to follow."

"I went to Hokkaido. Ask my block warden. I drank three glasses of wine, came home, fell on the front steps. It's all a matter of record; I was brought up and exonerated."

"So." Blake nodded. "Well, then. It's our contention that you met a woman; that you had met her before; that you have willingly and knowingly committed adultery with this woman."

"Thus collapses the juvenile system," Allen said bitterly. "Here ends empirical evidence. Back comes witch-burning. Hysterics and innuendo."

"You left your Agency," Blake continued, "on Tuesday of that week, to make a phone call from a public booth. It was a call you couldn't make in your office, for fear of being overheard."

"To this girl?" They were ingenious, at least. And they probably believed it. "What's the girl's name?"

"Grace Maldini," Blake said. "About twenty-four years old, standing five-foot-five, weighing about one twenty-five. Dark hair, dark skin, presumably of Italian extraction."

It was Gretchen, of course. Now he was really perplexed.

"On Thursday morning you were two hours late to work. You walked off and were lost along the commute lanes. You deliberately chose routes through the thickest traffic."

"Conjection," Allen said. But it had been true; he was on his way to the Health Resort. Grace Maldini? What on earth was that about?

"On Saturday morning of that week," Blake continued, "you did the same thing. You shook off anybody who might have been following you and met this girl at an unknown point. You did not return to your apartment that day. That night, a week ago yesterday, you boarded an inter-S ship in the company of the girl, who registered herself as Miss Grace Maldini. You registered under the name John Coates. When the ship reached Centaurus, you and the girl transferred to a second ship, and again you shook monitoring. You did not return to Earth during the entire week. It was within that period that your wife described you as 'completing work at your Agency.' This evening, about thirty minutes ago, you stepped off an inter-S ship, dressed as you are now, entered a phone booth, and then came here."

They were all looking at him, waiting with interest. This was an ultimate block meeting: avid curiosity, the need to hear every lurid detail. And, with that, the solemn Morec of duty.

At least he knew how he had been gotten from Earth to Other World. Malparto's therapeutic drugs had kept him docile, while Gretchen thought up names and made the arrangements. Four days in her company: the first emergence of John Coates.

"Produce the girl," Allen said.

Nobody spoke.

"Where is she?" They could look forever for Grace Maldini. And without her it was so much hearsay. "Let's see her. Where does she live? What's her lease? Where does she work? Where is she right now?"

Blake produced a photograph, and Allen examined it. A blurred print: he and Gretchen seated side by side in large chairs. Gretchen was reading a magazine and he was asleep. Taken on the ship, no doubt, from the other end of the lounge.

"Incredible," he mocked. "There I am, and a woman's sitting next to me."

Myron Mavis took the picture, studied it, and sneered. "Not worth a cent. Not worth the merest particle of a rusty Mexican cent. Take it back."

Mrs. Hoyt said thoughtfully: "Myron's right. This isn't proof of anything."

"Why did you assume the name Coates?" Luddy spoke up. "If you're so innocent —"

"Prove that, too," Mavis said. "This is ridiculous. I'm going home; I'm tired, and Purcell looks tired. Tomorrow is Monday and you know what that means for all of us."

Mrs. Frost arose, folded her arms, and said to Allen: "We all agree it isn't remotely possible to call this material *proof*. But it's disturbing. Evidently you did make the phone calls; you did go somewhere out of the ordinary; you have been gone the last week. What you tell me I'll believe. So will Mrs. Hoyt."

Mrs. Hoyt inclined her head.

"Have you left your wife?" Mrs. Frost asked. "One simple question. Yes or no."

"No," he said, and it was really, actually true. There was no lie involved. He looked her straight in the eye. "No adultery, no affair, no secret love. I went to Hokkaido and got material. I phoned a male friend." Some friend. "I visited the same friend. This last week has been an unfortunate involvement in circumstances beyond my control, growing out of my retiring from my Agency and accepting the directorship. My motives and actions have been in the public interest, and my conscience is totally clear."

Mrs. Hoyt said: "Let the boy go. So he can take a bath and get some sleep."

Her hand out, Sue Frost approached Allen. "I'm sorry, I am. You know that."

They shook, and Allen said: "Tomorrow morning, at eight?"

"Fine." She smiled sheepishly. "But we had to check. A charge of this sort — you understand."

He did. Turning to Blake and Luddy, who were stuffing their material back in its briefcase, Allen said: "Packet number 355-B. Faithful husband the victim of old women living in the housing unit who cook up a kettle of filth and then get it tossed in their faces."

Hurriedly, glancing down, Blake murmured good nights and departed. Luddy followed after him. Allen wondered how long the false lead would keep him alive.

16

HIS NEW OFFICE at Telemedia had been cleaned, swept, repainted, and his desk had been moved from the Agency as a gesture of continuity. By ten o'clock Monday morning, Allen had got the feel of things. He had sat in the big swivel chair, used the pencil sharpener, stood before the one-way viewing wall covertly surveyed his building-sized staff.

While he was stabilizing himself, Myron Mavis, looking as if he hadn't gone to bed, appeared to wish him luck.

"Not a bad layout," Mavis said. "Gets plenty of sunlight, good air. Very healthy; look at me."

"I hoped you're not selling your hoofs for glue," Allen said, feeling humble.

"Not for a while. Come on." Mavis guided him out of the office. "I'll introduce you to the staff."

They squeezed past the bundles of congratulatory "flowers" along the corridor. The reek of crypto-flora assailed them, and Allen halted to examine cards. "Like a hot house," he said. "Here's one from Mrs. Hoyt."

There was a bundle from Sue Frost, from Harry Priar, and from Janet. There were gaudy bundles from the four giant Agencies, including Blake-Moffet. All bore formal greetings. Their representatives would be in shortly. And there were unmarked bundles with no cards. He wondered who had sent them. Persons in the housing unit; perhaps little Mr. Wales who had stuck up for him during the block meeting. Others, from anonymous individuals who wished him luck. There was a dingy bunch, very small, which he picked up; some sort of blue growth.

"Those are real," Mavis said. "Smell them. Bluebells, I think they were called. Somebody must have dredged them up from the past."

Probably Gates and Sugermann. And one of the anonymous bundles could represent the Mental Health Resort. In the back of his mind was the conviction that Malparto would be seeking to recover his investment.

The staff quit work and lined up for his inspection. He shook hands, made random inquiries, spoke sage comments, greeted personnel he remembered. It was almost noon by the time he and Mavis had made the circuit of the building.

"That was kind of a bad scrape, last night," Mavis said, as they returned to the office. "Blake-Moffet has been after the directorship for years. It must hurt like hell to see you in."

Allen opened the file he had brought and rummaged for a packet. "Remember this?" He passed it to Mavis. "Everything started with this."

"Oh yes." Mavis nodded. "The tree that died. The anti-colonization Morec."

"You know better than that," Allen said.

Mavis looked bland. "Symbol of spiritual starvation, then. Severed from the folk-soul. You're going to put that through? The new Renaissance in propaganda. What Dante did for the afterworld, you're going to do for this."

"This particular packet," Allen said, "is long overdue. It should have come out months ago. I suppose I could start out cautiously, process only what's already been bought. Interfere with the staff as little as possible. Let them go the way they've been going — the low-risk approach." He opened the packet. "But."

"Not but." Mavis leaned close, put the side of his hand to his lips, and whispered hoarsely: "The watchword is *Excelsior.*"

He shook hands with Allen, wished him luck, hung lonelily around the building for an hour or so, and then was gone.

Watching Mavis shuffle off, Allen was conscious of his own burden. But the sense of weight made him cheerful.

"Seven with one blow," he said.

"Yes, Mr. Purcell," a battery of intercoms responded, as secretaries came to life.

"My father can lick your father," Allen said. "I'm just testing the equipment. You can go back to sleep, or whatever it is you're doing."

Removing his coat he settled himself at his desk and began dividing up the packet. There was still nothing in it he cared to alter, so he marked it "satisfactory" and tossed it in the basket. The basket whisked it off, and, somewhere down the long chain of command, the packet was received and put into process.

He picked up the phone and called his wife.

"Where are you?" she said, as if she was afraid to believe it. "Are you . . ."

"I'm there," he said.

"H-how's the job?"

"Power unlimited."

She seemed to relax. "You want to celebrate tonight?"

The idea sounded good. "Sure. This is our big triumph; we should enjoy it." He tried to think what would be appropriate. "I could bring home a quart of ice cream."

Janet said: "I'd feel better if you told me what happened last night with Mrs. Frost."

There was no point in giving her grounds for her anxiety.

"You worry too much. It came out all right, and that's what matters. This morning I put through the tree packet. Remember that? Now they can't bury it in dust. I'm going to transfer my best men from the Agency, men like Harry Priar. I'll trim down the staff here until I have something manageable."

"You won't make the projections too hard to understand, will you? I mean, don't put together things over people's heads."

"Nobody can say what's 'over people's heads,'" Allen said. "The aged-in-the-stalk formula material is on its way out, and all sorts of new stuff is coming in. We'll try a little of everything."

Wistfully, Janet said: "Remember how much fun it was when we started? Forming the Agency, hitting T-M with our new ideas, our new kind of packets."

He remembered. "Just keep thinking about that. I'll see you tonight. Everything's coming out fine, so don't worry." He added goodbye, and then hung up.

"Mr. Purcell," his desk intercom said, "there are a number of people waiting to see you."

"Okay, Doris," he said.

"Vivian, Mr. Purcell." What sounded like a giggle. "Shall I send the first one in?"

"Send him, her, or it in," Allen said. He folded his hands in front of him and scrutinized the door.

The first person was a woman, and she was Gretchen Malparto.

17

GRETCHEN WORE A tight blue suit, carried a beaded purse, was pale and drawn, dark-eyed with tension. She smelled of fresh flowers and looked beautiful and expensive. Closing the door, she said:

"I got your note."

"The baby was a boy. Six pounds." The office seemed filled with tiny drifting particles; he rested his palms against the desk and closed his eyes. When he opened his eyes the particles were gone but Gretchen was still there; she had seated herself, crossed her legs, and was fingering the edge of her skirt.

"When did you arrive back here?" she asked.

"Sunday night."

"I got in this morning." Her eyebrows wavered and across her face flitted a blind, crumpled pain. "You certainly walked right out."

"Well," he said, "I figured out where I was."

"Was it so bad?"

Allen said: "I can call people in here and have you tossed out. I can have you barred; I can have all kinds of things done to you. I can even have you arrested and prosecuted for a felony, you and your brother and that demented outfit you run. But that puts an end to me. Even Vivian walking in to take dictation is the end, with you sitting there."

"Who's Vivian?"

"One of my new secretaries. She comes along with the job."

Color had returned to Gretchen's features. "You're exaggerating."

Allen went over and examined the door. It had a lock, so he locked it. He then went to the intercom, pressed the button, and said: "I don't want to be disturbed."

"Yes, Mr. Purcell," Vivian's voice sounded.

Picking up the phone, Allen called his Agency. Harry Priar answered. "Harry," Allen said, "get over here to T-M in something, a sliver or a Getabout. Park as close as you can and then come upstairs to my office."

"What's going on?"

"When you're here, phone me from my secretary's desk. Don't use the intercom." He hung up, bent over, and ripped the intercom loose. "These things are natural taps," he explained to Gretchen.

"You're really serious."

"Bet you I am." He folded his arms, leaned against the side of the desk. "Is your brother crazy?"

She gulped. "He — is, in a sense. A mania, collecting. But they all have it. This Psi mysticism. There was such a blob on your -gram; it tipped him across."

"How about you?"

"I suppose I'm not so clever either." Her voice was thin, brittle. "I've had four days travelling in to think about it. As soon as I saw you were gone, I followed. I — really thought you'd come back to the house. Wishful thinking . . . it was so damn nice and cozy." Suddenly she lashed out furiously. "You stupid bastard!"

Allen looked at his watch and saw that Harry Priar would

be another ten minutes. Probably he was just now backing the sliver onto the roof field of the Agency.

"What are you going to do with me?" Gretchen said.

"Drive you out somewhere and dump you." He wondered if Gates could help. Maybe she could be detained at Hokkaido. But that was their gimmick. "Didn't it seem a little unfair to me?" he said. "I went to you for help; I acted in good faith."

Staring at the floor, Gretchen said: "My brother's responsible. I didn't know in advance; you were starting out the door to leave, and then you keeled over. He gas-pelleted you. Somebody was detailed to get you to Other World; they were going to ship you there by freight, in a cataleptic state. I—was afraid you might die. It's risky. So I accompanied you." She raised her head. "I wanted to. It was a terrible thing to do, but it was going to happen anyhow."

He felt less hostility, since it was probably true. "You're an opportunist," he murmured. "The whole affair was ingenious. Especially that bit when the house dissolved. What's this blob on my -gram?"

"My brother puzzled over it from the time he got it. He never figured it out, and neither did the Dickson. Some psionic talent. Precognition, he thinks. You japed the statue to prevent your own murder at the hands of the Cohorts. He thinks the Cohorts kill people who rise too high."

"Do you agree?"

"No," she said, "because I know what the blob means. You do have something in your mind nobody else has. But it's not precognition."

"What is it?"

Gretchen said: "You have a sense of humor."

The office was quiet as Allen considered and Gretchen sat smoothing her skirt.

"Maybe so," Allen said finally.

"And a sense of humor doesn't fit in with Morec. Or with us. You're not a 'mutant'; you're just a balanced human being." Her voice gained strength. "The japery, everything you've done. You're just trying to re-establish a balance in an unbalanced world. And it's something you can't even admit to yourself. On the top you believe in Morec. Underneath there's that blob, that irreducible core, that grins and laughs and plays pranks."

"Childish," he said.

"Not at all."

"Thanks." He smiled down at her.

"This is such a goddamn mess." From her purse she got her handkerchief; she wiped her eyes and then stuffed the handkerchief into her coat pocket. "You've got this job, Director of Telemedia, the high post of morality. Guardian of public ethics. You *create* the ethics. What a screwy, mixed-up situation."

"But I want this job."

"Yes, your ethics are very high. But they're not the ethics of this society. The block meetings—you loathe them. The faceless accusers. The juveniles—the busybody prying. This senseless struggle for leases. The anxiety. The tension and strain; look at Myron Mavis. And the overtones of guilt and suspicion. Everything becomes—tainted. The fear of contamination; fear of committing an indecent act. Sex is morbid; people hounded for natural acts. This whole structure is like a giant torture chamber, with everybody staring at one another, trying to find fault, trying to break one another down. Witchhunts and star chambers. Dread and censorship, Mr. Bluenose banning books. Children kept from hearing *evil*. Morec was invented by sick minds, and it creates more sick minds."

"All right," Allen said, listening. "But I'm not going to lie around watching girls sun-bathe. Like a salesman on vacation."

"That's all you see in the Resort?"

"That's all I see in Other World. And the Resort is a machine to process people there."

"It does more than that. It provides them with a place they can escape to. When their resentment and anxiety starts destroying them —" She gestured. "Then they go over."

"Then they don't smash store windows. Or jape statues. I'd rather jape statues."

"You came to us once."

"As I see it," Allen said, "the Resort acts as part of the system. Morec is one half and you're the other. Two sides of the coin: Morec is all work and you're the badminton and checkers set. Together you form a society; you uphold and support each other. I can't be in both parts, and of the two I prefer this."

"Why?"

"At least something's being done, here. People are working. You tell them to go out and fish."

"So you won't go back with me," she said reasonably. "I didn't really think you would."

"Then what did you show up here for?"

"To explain. So you'd understand how that whole damn foolish business happened, and what my part was. Why I got involved. And so you'd understand about yourself. I wanted you to be aware of your feelings — the hostility you feel toward Morec. The deep outrage you have for its cruelties. You're moving in the direction of integration. But I wanted to help. Maybe it'll pay you back for what we took. You did ask us for help. I'm sorry."

"Being sorry is a good idea," he said. "A step in the right direction."

Gretchen got up and put her hand on the doorknob. "I'll take the next step. Goodbye."

"Just sit down." He propelled her back to the chair but she disengaged her arm. "What now?" he demanded. "More speeches?"

"No." She faced him. "I give up. I won't cause you any more trouble. Go back to your little worrying wife; that's where you belong."

"She's younger than you," Allen said. "As well as smaller."

"How wonderful," Gretchen said lightly. "But — does she understand about you? This core you have that makes you different and keeps you out of the system? Can she help bring that out as it should be? Because that's important, more important than anything else. Even this heroic position, this new job, isn't really —"

"Still the welfare worker," he said. He was only partly listening to her; he was watching for Harry Priar.

"You do believe what I say, don't you? About you; about what's inside you."

"Okay," he said. "I'm taken in by your story."

"It's true. I — really care about you, Allen. You're a lot like Donna's father. Equivocating about the system, leaving it and then going back. The same doubts and mistrusts. Now he's back here for good. I said goodbye to him. I'm saying goodbye to you, the same way."

"One last thing," Allen said. "For the record. Do you honestly suppose I'm going to pay that bill?"

"It does seem stupid. There's a routine procedure, and it was marked 'for services rendered,' so nobody would identify it. I'll have the account voided." She was suddenly shy. "I'd like to ask for something. Possibly you'll laugh."

"Let's hear it."

"Why don't you kiss me goodbye?"

"I hadn't thought about it." He made no move.

Stripping off her gloves, Gretchen laid them with her purse

and raised her bare, slim fingers to his face. "There really isn't anybody named Molly, is there? You just made her up." She dug her nails into his neck, tugging him down against her. Her breath, as she kissed him, was faintly sweet with peppermint, and her lips were moist. "You're so good." she said, turning her face away.

She screamed.

On the floor of the office was a metal earwig-shaped creature, its receptor stalks high and whirring. The juvenile scuttled closer, then retreated in a dash of motion.

Allen grabbed up a paper weight from the desk and threw it at the juvenile. He missed, and the thing kept on going. It was trying to get back out the window, through which it had come. As it scooted up the wall he lifted his foot and smashed it; the juvenile fell broken to the floor and crawled in a half-circle. Allen found a typewriter and dropped it on the crippled juvenile. Then he began searching for its reservoir of tape.

While he was searching, the office door fell open and a second juvenile spurted in. Behind it was Fred Luddy, snapping pictures with a flash camera. With him were Blake-Moffet technicians, trailing wires and earphones and lenses and mikes and batteries. After the Blake-Moffet people came a horde of T-M employees, screeching and fluttering.

"Sue us for the lock!" Luddy shouted, tripping on a mike cable. "Somebody get the tape from that busted juve —"

Two technicians jumped past Gretchen and swept up the remains of the demolished juvenile. "Looks intact, Fred."

As Luddy snapped pictures, tape transports revolved and the surviving juvenile whirred exultantly. The office was jammed with people and equipment; Gretchen stood huddled in a corner, and somewhere far off burglar alarms were ringing.

"We reamed out the lock!" Luddy shouted, rushing up to Allen with his camera. "You didn't hear it; you were killing that juve we sent in through the window. Up six flights — those things *climb!*"

"Run," Allen said to Gretchen, pushing people out of her way. "Get downstairs and out of here."

She broke from her paralysis and started toward the open door. Luddy saw and yelped with dismay; he shoved his camera into a subordinate's arm and hurried after. As he caught hold of her arm, Allen reached him and socked him on the jaw. Luddy collapsed, and Gretchen, with a wail of despair, disappeared down the corridor.

"Oh boy," one of the Blake-Moffet's men chortled, helping Luddy up. "Have we got pictures."

There were now three juveniles, and more were on the way. Allen seated himself on an air conditioner and rested. Turmoil surged everywhere; the Blake-Moffet people were still taking pictures and his own T-M people were trying to restore order.

"Mr. Purcell," one of his secretaries — probably Vivian — was shrilling in his ear. "What'll we do? Call the police?"

"Get them out," Allen grunted. "Bring up people from the other departments and throw them out. They're trespassing."

"Yes sir," the secretary said, and darted off.

Luddy, propped up by two of his compatriots, approached. He was fingering his chin and he had got back his camera. "The first tape's intact. You and that gal clinching; it's all down. And the rest, too; you busting the juve up and hitting me, and send-ing her off. And the door locked, the intercom ripped out — the whole works."

From the confusion Harry Priar emerged. "What happened, Allen?" He saw Luddy and the juveniles. "Oh no," he said. "No."

"You didn't last long," Luddy said to Allen. "You —" He ducked off as Priar started at him.

"I guess," Priar said, "I didn't get here in time."

"How'd you come? On your hands?" Some of the chaos was

dying down. The Blake-Moffet people, and their equipment, were being forcibly ushered out. They were all smiles. His own staff was gathering in gloomy bunches, glancing at him and exchanging mutters. A T-M repairman was inspecting the hole in the office door where the lock had been. Blake-Moffet had carried the lock off with them, probably as a trophy.

"Invasion," Priar said. "I never would have thought Luddy had the guts."

"Blake's idea," Allen said. "And Luddy's vendetta. So now it comes full cycle. I got Luddy, now he gets me."

"Did they — I mean, they got what they wanted, didn't they?"

"Drums of it," Allen said. "I did the ultimate; I stamped on a juvenile."

"Who was the girl?"

Allen grimaced. "Just a friend. A niece visiting from the country. My daughter. Why do you ask?"

18

LATE THAT NIGHT he sat with Janet in the darkness, listening to the noises filtering through the walls from other apartments. The murmur of voices, faint music, rattle of dishes and pans, and indiscriminate globs of sound that could be anything.

"Want to go for a walk?" he asked.

"No." Janet stirred a little beside him.

"Want to go to bed?"

"No. Just sit."

Presently Allen said: "I ran into Mrs. Birmingham on my way to the bathroom. They brought the reports in a convoy of Getabouts. Six men guarding it. Now she's got it all hidden somewhere, probably in an old stocking."

"You're going into the block meeting?"

"I'll be there, and I'm going to fight with everything I've got."

"Will it do any good?"

He reflected. "No."

"Then," Janet said, "we're washed up."

"We'll lose our lease, if that's what you mean. But that's all Mrs. Birmingham can do. Her authority ends when we leave here."

"You've resigned yourself to that," Janet said.

"I might as well." He searched for his cigarettes, then gave up. "Haven't you?"

"Your family worked decades for this lease. All those years your mother was with the Sutton Agency before it merged. And your father in T-M's art department."

"Pooled status," he said. "You don't have to remind me. But I'm still Director of Telemedia. Maybe I can wangle a lease out of Sue Frost. Technically I'm entitled to one. We should be living in Myron Mavis' apartment, within walking distance of my work."

"Would she give you a lease now? After this business today?"

He tried to imagine Sue Frost and the expression on her face. The sound of her voice. The rest of the day he had hung around his office at T-M expecting her to call, but she hadn't. No word had arrived from above; the powers had remained mum.

"She'll be disappointed," he said. "Sue had the kind of hopes for me only a mother could invent."

Up the ladder generation by generation. The schemings of old women, the secret ambitions and activity of parents boosting their children one more notch. Exhaustion, sweat, the grave.

"We can assume Blake-Moffet briefed her," he said. "I guess it's time to tell you what happened last night at the apartment."

He told Janet, and she had nothing to say. There wasn't enough light in the apartment to see her face, and he wondered if she had passed out with wretchedness. Or if some primordial storm were going to burst over him. But, when he finally nudged her, she simply said: "I was afraid it was something like that."

"Why the hell why?"

"I just had a feeling. Maybe I'm clairvoyant." He had told her about Doctor Malparto's Psionic-testing. "And it was the same girl?"

"The girl who got me to the Health Resort; the girl who helped kidnap me; the girl who leaned her bosom in my face and said I was the father of her child. A very pretty black-haired girl with a big lovely house. But I did come back. Nobody seems to care about that part."

"I care," Janet said. "Do you think she was in on the frame-up?"

"The idea entered my mind. But she wasn't. There was nothing to be gained, except by Blake-Moffet. And the Resort isn't part of Blake-Moffet. Gretchen was just witless and irresponsible and full of feminine vigor. Young love, they call it. And the idealism of her calling. Her brother's the same way: idealism, for the benefit, of the patient."

"It's so sort of crazy," Janet protested. "All she did was walk into your office, and all you did was kiss her when she left. And you're completely ruined."

"The work is 'vile enterprise,'" Allen said. "It'll be showing up Wednesday, about nine A.M. I wonder what Mr. Wales can do in my defense. It should pose quite a challenge to him."

But the block meeting wasn't really important. The unknown was Sue Frost, and her reaction might not be in for days. After all, she had to confer with Ida Pease Hoyt: the reaction needed the stamp of absolute finality.

"Didn't you say something about bringing home a quart of ice cream?" Janet asked wanly.

"Seems sort of silly," Allen said. "Everything considered."

19

On wednesday morning the first-floor chamber of the housing unit was crammed to bursting. The gossip relay had carried the news to everybody, mostly through the wives. Stale cigarette smoke hung in its cloud and the air conditioning system was making no progress. At the far end was the platform on which the wardens sat, and they were all present.

In a freshly-starched dress, Janet entered slightly ahead of him. She went directly to a vacant table and placed herself before the microphone. The table, by an unverbalized protocol, was purposely untaken; in times of real crisis the wife was expected to aid her husband. To deprive her of that right would have been an affront to Morec.

Last time, no table had been left vacant. Last time had not been a crisis.

"This serious is," Allen said to his wife, stationing himself behind her. "And this long is; this vindictive is; and this going to lose is. So don't get too involved. Don't try to save me, because I can't be saved. As we said last night."

She nodded sightlessly.

"When they start burying their teeth in me," he continued softly, as if humming a tune, "don't spring up and take them all on. This is so rigged it's ready to burst. For example, where's little Mr. Wales?"

The man who had faith in Allen Purcell was not present. And the doors were being closed: he was not coming.

"They probably discovered a loophole in his lease," Allen said. Now Mrs. Birmingham was rising to her feet and accepting the agenda. "Or it turned out that he's the owner of a chain of whorehouses stretching from Newer York to Orionus."

Janet still continued to face front, with a rigidity he had never before seen. She seemed to have created an exoskeleton for herself, a containing envelope through which nothing entered and nothing escaped. He wondered if she were saving herself for one grand slam. Perhaps it would appear when the ladies read their decision.

"It's dusty in here," Allen said, as the room dwindled into silence. A few persons glanced at him, then looked away. Since he was coasting downhill it was a poor idea to associate themselves with him.

At the end of the room the juveniles were surrendering their tapes. Seven tapes in all. Six, he conjectured, were for him. And one for everybody else.

"We will first undertake the case of Mr. A. P.," Mrs. Birmingham announced.

"Fine," Allen said, relieved. Again heads turned, then swiveled back. A murmur drifted up and joined the haze of cigarette smoke.

In a sardonic way he was amused. The rows of solemn, righteous faces . . . this was a church, and these were the members of the congregation in pious session. With long strides he made his way to the defendant's stage, hands in his pockets. In the rear, at her table, Janet sat wooden-faced, as stiff and unyielding as a carved stick. He nodded to her, and the session began.

. . .

"Mr. A. P.," Mrs. Birmingham said, in her noisy, authoritative voice, "did willingly and knowingly on the afternoon of October 22, 2114, in his place of business and during the working hours of the day, engage in a vile enterprise with a young woman. Further, Mr. A. P. did willingly and knowingly destroy an official monitoring instrument to avoid detection, and to further avoid detection he did strike the face of a Morec citizen, damage private property, and in every possible fashion seek to conceal his actions."

A series of clicks bounced from the loudspeaker, as the voice warmed up. The interconnecting network was in operation: the speaker hummed, buzzed and then spoke.

"Definition. Be specific. Vile enterprise."

Mrs. Birmingham adjusted her glasses and read on. "Mr. A. P. did welcome the young woman — not his lawful wife — into his office at the Committee Telemedia Trust, and there he did lock himself in with her, did take precautions to guarantee that he not be discovered, and, when discovered, *was in the act of petting and embracing and sexually fondling the young woman about the shoulder and face*, and had so placed his body *that it was in contact with that of hers.*"

"Is this the same Mr. A. P. who was up before us the week before last?" the voice asked.

"It is," Mrs. Birmingham said, without reluctance.

"And this last week he was not present at the meeting?" The voice then declared: "Mr. A. P. is not being judged for his absence last week, and his lapse of the previous week has already been dealt with by this gathering."

The mood of the gathering was now varied. As always, many of the members were curious; some were bored and not particularly concerned. A few appeared unusually interested, and it was those to whom Allen paid attention.

"Mr. A. P.," the voice said. "Was this the first time you had met the young woman?"

"No," he said. "I'd seen her before." It was a trap, practiced as a matter of routine: if his reply was that yes, this was the first time, he was open for the charge of promiscuity. Sexual misconduct was better understood if it was confined to one partner; Miss J. E. had been cleared by that point, and he intended to use it, too.

"Often?" the voice asked, infinitely toneless.

"Not in excess. We were good friends. We still are. I think a great deal of Miss G. M. I have the highest respect for her, and so does my wife."

"Your wife knows her?" the voice asked. It answered its own question: "He just said so."

Allen said: "Let me make this clear. Miss G. M. is a responsible woman, and I have absolute faith in her moral integrity. Otherwise I wouldn't have admitted her to my office." His job was a matter of public knowledge, so he took the plunge. "In my position as Director of Telemedia, I must be highly careful of my choice of friends. Therefore —"

"How long have you been director?"

He hesitated. "Monday was my first day."

"And that was the day this young woman appeared?"

"People streamed in and out all day. Bundles of 'flowers' arrived; you're familiar with the protocol of congratulation. I was besieged by well-wishers. Miss G. M. was one of them. She dropped by to wish me luck."

The voice said: "A great *deal* of luck." Several persons smirked knowingly. "You locked the door, did you? You ripped out the intercom? You phoned for a Getabout to pick the two of you up as soon as possible?"

To his knowledge this information wasn't available on the official report. He felt uneasy. "I locked the door because people had been barging in all day. I was nervous and irritable. Frankly, I was a little overwhelmed by the job, and I didn't care to see anybody. As to the intercom —" He lied shamelessly, without conscience. Under the system there was no choice. "Being unfamiliar with my new office I inadvertently tripped over the wires. The wires broke. Anybody in business is aware that such things happen frequently — and at exactly such times."

"Indeed," the voice said.

"Miss G. M.," Allen went on, "stayed about ten minutes. When the monitoring device entered, I was saying goodbye to her. As she left she asked if she could kiss me, as a token of congratulation. Before I could say no, she had done so. That was what happened, and that was what the monitor saw."

"You tried to destroy the monitor."

"Miss G. M. screamed; she was taken unawares. It had entered by the window and neither of us noticed it. To be honest, we both imagined it was some sort of menace. I'm not clear now as to exactly what I thought it was. I heard Miss G. M. scream; I saw a blur of motion. Instinctively I kicked out, and my foot connected with it."

"This man you hit."

"At Miss G. M.'s scream the door was forced and a number of hysterical people burst in. There was bedlam for a time, which is reported. A man ran up and started to grab at Miss G. M. I thought it was an attack aimed at Miss G. M., and I had no choice but to defend her. As a gentleman it was incumbent on me."

"Does the record bear that out?" the voice asked.

Mrs. Birmingham consulted. "The individual who was struck was attempting physically to apprehend the young woman." She turned a page. "However, it is stated that Mr. A. P. had instructed the woman to flee the scene."

"Naturally," Allen said. "Since I feared an attack on her I wanted her to escape to safety. Consider the situation. Miss G. M. enters, my office to wish me —"

"This is the same Miss G. M.," the voice interrupted, "with whom you spent four days and *nights* on an inter-S ship? The same Miss G. M. who registered under a phony name in order to conceal her identity? Is this not the same Miss G. M. with whom you have committed adultery at a number of times, in a number of places? Is it not true that all this has been concealed from your wife and that in reality your wife has never met this woman and could not possibly have any opinion of her except the normal opinion of a wife toward her husband's mistress?"

General pandemonium.

Allen waited for the noise to die down. "I have never committed adultery with anybody. I have no romantic relationship with Miss G. M. I have never —"

"You fondled her; you kissed her; don't you call that romantic?"

"Any man," Allen said, "who is capable of sexual activity during his first day at a new job is an unusual man."

Appreciative laughter. And a scatter of applause.

"Is Miss G. M. pretty?" This, in all probability, was a wife. The planted questioner, with extra information at his disposal, had temporarily retired.

"I suppose," Allen said. "Now that I think of it. Yes, she was attractive. Some men would think so."

"When did you first meet her?"

"Oh, about —" And then he broke off. He had almost fallen on that one. Two weeks was the wrong answer. No friendship of two weeks included a hug and kiss, in the Morec world. "I'll have to think back," he said, as if it were decades. "Let's see, when I first met her I was working for . . ." He let his voice trail off, until the questioner became impatient and asked:

"How did you meet her?"

In the back of his mind Allen sensed that the enemy was closing in. There were many questions he couldn't answer, questions for which no evasion would work. This was one of them.

"I don't remember," he said, and saw the floor open to receive him. "Some mutual friends, maybe."

"Where does she work?"

"I don't know."

"Why did you take a four-day trip with her?"

"Prove that I did." He had the way out of that, at least. "Is that in the report?"

Mrs. Birmingham searched, and shook her head no

"Mr. A. P.," the voice said, "I'd like to ask you this." He couldn't tell if this were the same accuser; warily, he assumed it was. "Two weeks ago, when you arrived home drunk. Had you been with this woman?"

"No," he said, which was true.

"Are you positive? You had been alone at your office; you took a sliver to Hokkaido; you showed up several hours later clearly having had —"

"I didn't even know her then," he said. And realized his utter and final mistake. But now, alas, it was too late.

"You met her less than *two weeks ago?*"

"I had seen her before." His voice came out insect-frail, weak with awareness of defeat. "But I didn't know her well."

"What happened between you and her during the last two weeks? Was that when the relationship grew?"

Allen reflected at length. No matter how he answered, the situation was hopeless. But it was bound to end this way. "I'm not aware," he said at last, half-idly, "that it ever grew, then or any other time."

"To you a relationship with a young woman not your wife that involves petting and fondling and the juxtaposition of bodies —"

"To a diseased mind any relationship is foul," Allen said. He got to his feet and faced the people below him. "I'd like to see who I'm talking to. Come on out from under your rock; let's see what you look like."

The impersonal voice went on: "Are you in the habit of putting your hands on the bodies of young women with whom you happen, during the course of the day, to come in contact? Do you use your job as a means by which—"

"I tell you what," Allen said. "If you'll identify yourself I'll knock the living Jesus out of you. I'm fed-up with this faceless accusation. Obscene, sadistic minds are using these meetings to pry out all the sordid details, tainting every harmless act by pawing over it, reading filth and guilt into every normal human relationship. Before I step off this stage I have one general, theoretical statement to make. The world would be a lot better place if there was no morbid inquisition like this. More harm is done in one of these sessions than in all the copulation between man and woman since the creation of the world."

He reseated himself. No sound was audible anywhere. The room was totally silent. Presently Mrs. Birmingham said: "Unless anybody wishes to make any further statements, the Council will prepare its decision."

There was no response from the impersonal voice of "justice." Allen, hunched over, realized that it had said not one word in his defense. Janet still sat like a stick of wood. Possibly she agreed with the accusations. At the moment it didn't really matter to him.

The council of ladies conferred for a period that seemed to him unnecessarily long. After all, the decision was foregone. He plucked at a thread on his sleeve, coughed, twisted restlessly on the chair. At last Mrs. Birmingham stood.

"The block-neighbors of Mr. A. P." she stated, "regret that they are required to find Mr. A. P. to be an undesirable tenant.

This exceptionally unfortunate is, since Mr. A. P. has been an exemplary tenant in this housing unit for many years, and his family before him. Mr. A. P., in point of fact, was born in the apartment he now holds. Therefore it is with deep reluctance that the Council, speaking for Mr. A. P.'s block-neighbors, declares his lease to be void as of the sixth day of November, 2114, and with even deeper reluctance petitions Mr. A. P. to remove his person, family, and possessions from these premises by that date." Mrs. Birmingham was silent a moment and then concluded: "It is also hoped that Mr. A. P. will understand that given the circumstances the Council and his block-neighbors had no choice in the matter, and that they wish him the best of personal luck. In addition, the Council wishes to make clear its conviction that Mr. A. P. is a man of greatest fortitude and perseverance, and it is the Council's belief that Mr. A. P. will surmount this temporary difficulty."

Allen laughed out loud.

Mrs. Birmingham glanced at him quizzically, then folded up her statement and stepped back. Allen walked from the stage, down the steps and across the crowded room to the table at which his wife sat.

"Come on," he said to her. "We might as well leave."

As the two of them pushed outside they heard Mrs. Birmingham droning into the next indictment.

"We will now undertake the case of R. P., a boy, age nine, who did willingly and knowingly on the morning of October 21, 2114, scrawl certain pornographic words on the wall of the community bathroom of the second floor of this housing unit."

"Well," Allen said to his wife, as the door was locked after them, "that's that."

She nodded.

"How do you feel?" he asked.

"It seems so unreal."

"It's real. We have two weeks to get out. Temporary difficulty." He shook his head. "What a travesty."

Loitering in the corridor was Mr. Wales, a folded newspaper under his arm. As soon as he saw Allen and Janet he walked hesitantly forward. "Mr. Purcell."

Allen halted. "Hello, Mr. Wales. We missed you."

"I wasn't in there." Mr. Wales seemed both apologetic and animated. "Mr. Purcell, my new lease came through. That's why I wasn't there; I'm not part of this unit any more."

"Oh," Allen said. So they hadn't eased him out; they had bought up a superior lease and presented it to him. Presumably Mr. Wales was ignorant of the purpose of his good fortune; after all, he had his own problems.

"What was it like in there?" Mr. Wales asked. "Somebody told me you were up again."

"I was," Allen admitted.

"Serious?" Mr. Wales was concerned.

"Not too serious." Allen patted the little fellow on the arm. "It's all over now."

"I hope because I wasn't—"

"Made no difference at all. But thanks anyhow."

They shook hands. "Drop by and see us," Mr. Wales said. "My wife and I. We'd be glad to have you."

"Okay," Allen said, "we'll do that. When we're in the neighborhood."

After returning Janet to the apartment, Allen walked the long way to Telemedia and his new office. His staff was subdued; they greeted him and swiftly returned to their work. His two-hour absence testified to a block meeting; they all knew where he had been.

In his office he examined a summary of the day's schedule.

The tree packet was in process, and for that he was glad. He called a few T-M officials in, discussed technical problems, then sat alone for a while, smoking and meditating.

At eleven-thirty Mrs. Sue Frost, in a long coat, looking handsome and efficient, bustled cheerfully in to pay a visit.

"I won't take up much of your time," she announced. "I realize how busy you are."

"Just sitting here," he murmured. But she went on:

"We were wondering if you and your wife are free, tonight. I'm having a little Juggle get-together at my place, just a few people; we'd particularly like, you two to be there. Mavis will be there, so will Mrs. Hoyt and perhaps —"

He interrupted: "You want my resignation? Is that it?"

Flushing, she said: "As long as we're going to be getting together I thought it might be a good opportunity to discuss further some of the —"

"Let's have a direct answer," he said.

"All right," she said. In a tight, controlled voice she said, "We'd like your written resignation."

"When?"

"As soon as possible."

He said, "You mean now?"

With almost perfect composure Sue Frost said, "Yes. If it's convenient."

"What if it isn't?"

For a moment she did not seem to understand.

"I mean," he said, "what if I refuse to resign?"

"Then," she said, facing him calmly, "you'll be discharged."

"As of when?"

Now, for the first time, she floundered. "Mrs. Hoyt will have to approve. As a matter of fact —"

"As a matter of fact," he said, "it takes full Committee action.

My lease is good until the sixth and it'll be at least that long before you can legally get me out of T-M. Meanwhile I'm still Director. If you want me you can call me here at my office."

"You're serious?" she said, in a strained voice.

"I am," Allen said. "Has this ever happened before?"

"N-no."

"I didn't think so." He picked up some papers from his desk
and began to study them; in the time he had left there was a
great deal of work to be done.

20

ALL ALONE, MR. WALES surveyed his new apartment in unit R6 of leasing zone 28. A lifelong dream was fulfilled. He had advanced not one but two zones toward *omphalos*. The Housing Authority had investigated his petition, seen the utter virtue of his life, his devotion to public good.

Moving about the room, Mr. Wales touched walls, the floor, gazed out the window, inspected the closet. He ran his hands over the stove, marveling at his gain. The former tenants had even left their Edufactured objects: clock, shaving wand, small appliances.

To Mr. Wales it seemed unbelievable that his trivial person had been recognized. Petitions lay in ten-foot heaps on the desks at the Housing Authority. Surely there was a God. Surely this proved that the gentle and the meek, the unassuming won out in the end.

Seating himself, Mr. Wales opened a package and brought forth a vase. He had acquired it as a gift for his wife, a celebration present. The vase was green and blue and speckled with light. Mr. Wales turned it around, blew on the smooth glazed surface, held it tightly in his hands.

Then he thought about Mr. Purcell. He remembered all the times Mr. Purcell had stuck up for victims in the weekly block meetings. All the kind words he had put in. The encouragement he had given the tormented in their trial.

Mr. Wales thought how Allen Purcell must have looked coming up before the last block meeting. The dogs tearing at him. The female bitches guzzling at his throat.

Suddenly Mr. Wales shouted: "I betrayed him! I let them crucify him!"

Anguished, he rocked back and forth. Then he sprang to his feet and hurled the vase against the wall. The vase burst, and bits of green and blue and speckled light danced around him.

"I'm a Judas," Mr. Wales said to himself. He covered his eyes with his fingers so he would not have to look at the apartment. He hated the apartment. Now he had what he had always wanted, and he didn't want it.

"I've changed my mind!" he shouted. But nobody heard him. "You can have it back!"

The room was silent.

"Go away!" Mr. Wales cried.

He opened his eyes. The room was still there. It did not respond; it did not leave.

Mr. Wales began gathering up the fragments of vase. The bits of glass cut his fingers. He was glad.

21

THE NEXT MORNING Allen arrived promptly at eight o'clock at his office in the Telemedia building. As the staff appeared for work, he called them into his office until all thirty-three of them were present. The hundreds of assignment workers continued at their desks throughout the building as Allen addressed their executive department heads.

"Yesterday my resignation was requested. It's involved with the fracas that took place here Monday afternoon. I refused to resign, so I'm still Director, at least until the Committee can assemble and fire me."

The staff took the news with aplomb. One member, head of the layout department, asked: "How long will you remain in your estimation?"

"A week or so," Allen answered. "Maybe a little longer."

"And you intend to continue work during that time?"

"I'll work to the best of my ability," Allen said. "There's plenty to do and I want to get into it. But you're entitled to know the situation."

Another member of the staff, a trim woman with glasses, asked: "You're the legal Director, is that correct? Until they fire you —"

"Until dismissal papers are served, I'm the sole legal Director of this Trust; I'm your boss, with the powers implicit and explicit in that capacity. Naturally my policies here will be highly suspect. Probably the next Director will cancel them all, straight across the board."

The staff murmured among themselves.

"You should meditate over that," Allen said, "as I give you your assignments. How much trouble you'll get into for obeying and working with me I can't say. Your guess is as good as mine. Maybe the next Director will fire the lot of you. Probably not."

"It's unlikely," a staff member said.

"I'm going to give you a few hours to talk it over among yourselves. Let's say until noon. Those of you who would prefer not to take the risk can go home and wait out the period of my directorship. I'm positive that won't get you into trouble with the Committee; they may even suggest it."

One staff member asked: "What are your policies going to be? Maybe we should hear them before we decide."

"I don't think you should," Allen said. "You should make your decision on other grounds. If you stay, you'll have to follow my orders no matter what they are. This is the important thing for you to decide: do you care to work for a man who's out of favor?"

The staff left his office, and he was alone. Outside in the corridor their mumbles reached him dully through the closed door.

By noon virtually all the department heads had discreetly gone home. He was without an executive staff. The various operations went on, but the ranks were thinning. An unearthly loneliness hung around the building. The din of machines echoed in the empty offices and halls, and nobody seemed to feel like talking.

To the intercom he said: "Vivian, come in here a moment."

A rather drab young woman entered with pencil and pad.

"Yes, Mr. Purcell. My name is Nan, Mr. Purcell. Vivian left."

"You're staying?" he asked.

"Yes sir." She put on her thick glasses and made ready to take dictation.

"I want you to canvass the departments. It's noon, so presumably those remaining will be with us during the next week. Find out where the depletions are."

"Yes sir." She scribbled notes.

"Specifically I'll need to know which departments can function and which can't. Then send me the highest ranking staff member left. If no staff members are left, send in whoever you think is most familiar with general operations."

"Yes sir." She departed. An hour later a tall, gangling middle-aged party entered shyly.

"Mr. Purcell," he said. "I'm Gleeby. They said you wanted me. I'm head of music." He tilted his right ear with his thumb, conveying the interesting bit of news that he was deaf.

"Sit down," Allen said, pleased by the man, and pleased, also, that one of the staff remained. "You were in here at eight? You heard my speech?"

"Yes. I heard." Evidently the man lip-read.

"Well? Can we function?"

Gleeby pondered and lit his pipe. "Well, that's hard to say. Some departments are virtually closed down. We can redistribute personnel. Try to even up the losses. Fill in some of the widest gaps."

Allen asked: "Are you really prepared to carry out my orders?"

"Yes. I am." Gleeby sucked on his pipe.

"You may be held Morecly responsible."

"I'd become psychotic loafing around my apartment a week. You don't know my wife."

"Who here does the research?"

Gleeby was puzzled. "The Agencies handle that."

"I mean real research. Checking for historical accuracy. Isn't machinery set up to go over projections point by point?"

"A gal named Phyllis Frame does that. She's been around here thirty years. Has a big desk down in the basement, millions of files and records."

"Did she leave? If not, send her up."

Miss Frame hadn't left, and presently she appeared. She was a heavy, sturdy-looking, iron-haired lady, formidable and taciturn. "You wanted me, Director?"

"Be seated." He offered her his cigarette case, which she declined. "You understand the situation?"

"What situation?"

He explained. "So bear that in mind."

"I'll bear it in mind. What is it you want? I'm in a hurry to get back to my work."

"I want," Allen said, "a complete profile of Major Streiter. Not derived from packets or projections, but the actual facts as are known about his life, habits, character, and so forth. I want unbiased material. No opinions. Material that is totally authentic."

"Yes, Director."

"How soon can you have the profile?"

"By six." She was starting from the office. "Should this project include material on the Major's immediate family?"

Allen was impressed. "Yes. Very good."

"Thank you, Director." The door closed and she was gone.

At two o'clock Gleeby re-appeared with the final list of workers remaining. "We could be worse off. But there's almost nobody capable of making decisions." He rattled the list. "Give these people something to do and they'll go into action. But what'll we give them?"

"I have some ideas," Allen said.

After Gleeby had left the office, Allen phoned his old Agency.

"I have vacancies here," he said, "that need to be filled. I think I'll draw from the Agency. I'll put our people on the T-M payroll and try to get funds from the paymaster. If not, then I'll cover with Agency funds. Anyhow, I want people over here, and I'm sending my want-list to you."

"That'll deplete us," Harry Priar pointed out.

"Sure. But it's only for a week or so. Give our people the situation about me, see who's willing to come. Then fill as best you can. A dozen should do. What about you personally?"

"I'll work for you," Priar said.

"I'm in big disfavor."

Priar said: "When they ask, I'll say you brainwashed me."

Toward four in the afternoon the first trickle of Agency personnel began to show up. Gleeby interviewed each person and assigned him to a department. By the end of the day a makeshift working staff had been built up. Gleeby was optimistic.

"These are policy-making people," he said to Allen. "And they're used to working with you. We can trust them, too. Which good is. I suppose the Committee has a few of its creatures lurking around. Want us to set up some sort of loyalty review board?"

"Not important," Allen said. "As long as we see the finished products." He had studied the statement of projections in process; some were now scratched off, some had been put ahead, and most had been rerouted into dead-ends. The assembly lines were open and functioning, ready to undertake fresh material.

"What's that?" Gleeby asked, as Allen brought out sheets of lined paper.

"My preliminary sketches. What's the normal span required from first stage to last?"

"Well," Gleeby said, "say a packet is approved on Monday. Usually we take anywhere from a month to five months, depending on the medium it's to be projected over."

"Jesus," Allen said.

"It can be cut. For topical stuff we prune down to —" He computed. "Say, two weeks."

Allen turned to Harry Priar, who stood listening. "How's that strike you?"

"By the time you're out of here," Priar said, "you won't have one item done."

"I agree," Allen said. "Gleeby, to be on the safe side we'll have to prune to four days."

"That only happened once," Gleeby said, tugging at the lobe of his ear. "The day William Pease, Ida Pease Hoyt's father, died. We had a huge projection, on all media, within twenty-four hours."

"Even woven baskets?"

"Baskets, handbills, stenciled signs. The works."

Priar asked: "Anybody else going to be with us? Or is this the total crew?"

"I have a couple more people," Allen said. "I won't be sure until tomorrow." He looked at his watch. "They'd be at the top, as original idea men."

"Who are they?" Gleeby asked. "Anybody we know?"

"One of them is named Gates," he said, "The other is a man named Sugermann."

"Suppose I asked you what you're going to do?"

Allen said: "I'd tell you. We're going to do a jape on Major Streiter."

He was with his wife when the first plug was aired. At his direction a portable TV receiver was set up in their one-room apartment. The time was twelve-thirty at night; most of Newer York was asleep.

"The transmitting antenna," he told Janet, "is at the T-M building." Gleeby had collected enough video technicians to put the transmitter — normally closed down at that hour — back on the air.

"You're so excited," Janet said. "I'm glad you're doing this; it means so much to you."

"I only hope we can pull it off," he said, thinking about it.

"And afterward?" she said. "What happens then?"

"We'll see," he said. The plug was unfolding.

A background showed the ruins of the war, the aftermath of battle. The tattered rags of a settlement appeared; slow, halting motion of survivors creeping half-starved, half-baked through the rubble.

A voice said: "In the public interest a Telemedia discussion program will shortly deal with a problem of growing importance for our times. Participants will analyze the question. Should Major Streiter's postwar policy of active assimilation be revived to meet the current threat? Consult your area log for time and date."

The plug dissolved, carrying the ruins and desolation with it. Allen snapped off the TV set, and felt tremendous pride.

"What'd you think of it?" he asked Janet.

"Was that it?" She seemed disappointed. "There wasn't much."

"With variations, that plug will be repeated every half hour on all channels. Mavis' hit 'em, hit 'em. Plus plants in the newspapers, mentions on all the news programs, and minor hints scattered over the other media."

"I don't remember what 'active assimilation' was. And what's this 'current threat'?"

"By Monday you'll have the whole story," Allen said. "The slam will come on 'Pageant of Time.' I don't want to spoil it for you."

Downstairs on the public rack, he bought a copy of tomorrow's newspaper, already distributed. There, on page one, in the left-hand column, was the plant developed by Sugermann and Priar.

TALK OF REVIVING ASSIMILATION

Newer York Oct 29 (T-M): It is reliably reported that a number of persons high in Committee circles who prefer to remain anonymous at this time, favor a revival of the postwar policy of active assimilation developed by Major Streiter to cope with the then-extensive threats to Moral Reclamation. Growing out of the current menace this revived interest in assimilation expresses the continued uneasiness of violence and lawlessness, as demonstrated by the savage assault on the Park of the Spire monument to Major Streiter. It is felt that the therapeutic method of Mental Health, and the efforts of the Mental Health Resort to cope with current instability and unrest, have failed to

Allen folded up the newspaper and went back upstairs to the apartment. Within a day or so the domino elements of the Morec society would be tipped. "Active assimilation" as a solution to the "current threat" would be the topic of discussion for everybody.

"Active assimilation" was his brain child. He had made it up. Sugermann had added the idea of the "current threat." Between them they had created the topic out of whole cloth.

He felt well-pleased. Progress was being made.

22

BY MONDAY MORNING the projection was complete. T-M workers, armed, carried it upstairs to the transmitter and stood guard over it. The Telemedia building was sealed off; nobody came and nobody went. During the day the hints, spots, mentions on various media dinned like pond frogs. Tension began to build, a sense of expectancy. The public was alive to the topic of "active assimilation," although nobody knew what it meant.

"Opinion," Sugermann said, "runs about two to one in favor of restoring a cautious policy of active assimilation." A poll had been taken, and the results were arriving.

"Active assimilation's too good for those rascals," Gates announced. "Let's have no coddling of traitors."

At a quarter of eight that evening. Allen assembled his staff in his office. The mood was one of optimism.

"Well," Allen said, "it won't be long. Another fifteen minutes and we're on the air. Anybody feel like backing out?"

Everybody grinned inanely.

"Got your dismissal notice yet?" Gates asked him.

The notice, from the Committee, had arrived registered mail. Now Allen opened the envelope and read the brief, formal statement. He had until noon Thursday. Then he was no longer Director of Telemedia.

"Give me the story on the follow-ups," he said to Gleeby.

"Pardon? Yes, um." From a prepared list Gleeby read him the total projected coverage. "Up to now it's been ground breakers. Tonight at eight comes the actual discussion. Tomorrow night a repeat of the discussion program will be aired, by 'public demand.'"

"Better move that up," Allen said. "Allows too much time for them to act."

"Make it later tonight," Sugermann suggested. "About ten, as they're all popping into bed."

Gleeby scribbled a few words. "We've already mailed out duplicate films to the colonies. The discussion has been written up and will be printed in full in Tuesday morning's newspapers, plus comments pro and con. Late news programs tonight will give resumes. We've had the presses run off paper-bound copies to be sold in commissaries at magazine slots. Youth editions for school use have been prepared, but frankly, I don't imagine we can distribute them in time. It'll take another four days."

"And the poll," Sugermann added.

"Fine," Allen said. "For less than a week that's not bad."

A T-M employee entered. "Mr. Purcell, something's come up. Secretary Frost and Mrs. Hoyt are outside in a Committee Getabout. They want to be admitted."

"Peace party," Priar said.

"I'll talk to them outside," Allen said. "Show me where they are."

The employee led him to the ground floor and outside through the barricade erected before the entrance. In the back seat of a small blue Getabout sat the two women, bolt-upright, their faces pinched. Ralf Hadler was behind the tiller. He pretended not to notice or in any way conceive of Allen. They were not in the same world.

"Hi," Allen said.

Mrs. Hoyt said: "This unworthy is. I'm ashamed of you, Mr. Purcell. I really am."

"I'll make a note of that," Allen said. "What else?"

"Would you have the decency to tell us what you're doing?" Sue Frost demanded in a low, choked voice. She held up a news-paper. "'Active assimilation.' What in the name of heaven is this? Have you all completely lost your minds?"

"We have," Allen admitted. "But I don't see that it matters."

"It's a fabrication, isn't it?" Sue Frost accused. "You're in-venting it all. This is some sort of horrible prank. If I didn't know better I'd say you had a hand in the japery of Major Streit-er's statue; I'd say you're involved in this whole outbreak of an-archistic and savage lawlessness."

Her choice of words showed the potency of the campaign. It made him feel odd to hear her speaking right out of the plug.

"Now look," Mrs. Hoyt said presently, in a tone of forced amiability. "If you'll resign we'll see that you regain your lease. You'll be able to continue your Agency; you'll be exactly where you were. We'll prepare a guarantee, written, that Telemedia will buy from you." She hesitated. "And we'll undertake to ex-pose Blake-Moffet for their part in the frame-up."

Allen said: "Now I know I'm on the right track. And try to watch TV tonight; you'll get the full story on 'active assimilation.'"

Re-entering the building he halted to watch the blue Ge-tabout steam away. Their offer had genuinely surprised him. It was amazing how much moral righteousness the breath of scandal could blow down. He ascended by the elevator and joined the group waiting in his office.

"Almost time," Sugermann said, consulting his watch. "Five more minutes."

"At a rough guess," Gleeby said, "dominos representing seventy percent of the population will be watching. We should achieve an almost perfect saturation on this single airing."

From a suitcase Gates produced two fifths of Scotch whiskey. "To celebrate," he said, opening both. "Somebody get glasses. Or we can pass them around."

The phone rang, and Allen answered it.

"Hello, Allen," Myron Mavis' creaky voice came. "How're things going?"

"Absolutely perfect," Allen answered. "Want to stop by and join us?"

"Sorry. Can't. I'm bogged down in leaving. All my stuff to get packed for the trip to Sirius."

"Try to catch the projection tonight," Allen said. "It starts in a couple of minutes."

"How's Janet?"

"Seems to be feeling pretty fair. She's glad it's out in the open." He added, "She's watching at the apartment."

"Say hello to her," Mavis said. "And good luck on your lunacy."

"Thanks," Allen said. He said goodbye and hung up.

"Time," Sugermann said. Gates turned on the big TV receiver and they gathered around it. "Here we go."

"Here we go," Allen agreed.

Mrs. Georgina Birmingham placed her favorite chair before her television set and anticipated her favorite program, "The Pageant of Time." She was tired from the hectic activities of the day, but a deep spiritual residuum reminded her that work and sacrifice were their own reward.

On the screen was an inter-program announcement. A large decayed tooth was shown, grimacing with pain. Next to it a sparkling healthy tooth jeered sanctimoniously. The two teeth

engaged in Socratic dialogue, the upshot of which was the rout
and defeat of the bad tooth.

Mrs. Birmingham gladly endured the inter-program an-
nouncements because they were in a good cause. And the program, "Pageant of Time," was well worth any reasonable effort.
She always hurried home early on Monday evening; in ten years
she hadn't missed an edition.

A shower of brightly-colored fireworks burst across the
screen, and from the speaker issued the rumble of guns. A jag-
ged, slashing line of words cut through the blur of war:

THE PAGEANT OF TIME

Her program had begun. Folding her arms, leaning her head
back, Mrs. Birmingham now found herself viewing a table at
which sat four dignified gentlemen. A discussion was in progress, and dim words were audible. Over them was superimposed the announcer's voice.

"Pageant of Time. Ladies and gentlemen, at this table sit
four men, each a distinguished authority in his field. They had
come together to discuss an issue vital to every citizen of the
Morec society. In view of the unusual importance of this program there will be no interruptions, and the discussion, which
is already in progress, will proceed without pause until the end
of the hour. Our topic for tonight . . ." Visible words grew on the
screen.

ACTIVE ASSIMILATION IN THE WORLD TODAY

Mrs. Birmingham was delighted. She had been hearing about
active assimilation for some time, and this was her opportunity
to learn once and for all what it was. Her lack of information
had made her feel out of touch.

"Seated at my right is Doctor Joseph Gleeby, the noted educator, lecturer, writer of numerous books on problems of social values." A lean middle-aged man, smoking a pipe and rubbing his ear, was shown. "To Doctor Gleeby's right is Mr. Harold Priar, art critic, architect, frequent contributor to the *Encyclopedia Britannica*." A smaller individual was shown, with an intense, serious face. "Seated next to Mr. Priar is Professor Sugermann, whose historical studies rank with those of Gibbon, Schiller, Toynbee. We are very fortunate to have Professor Sugermann with us." The camera moved forth to show Professor Sugermann's heavy, solemn features. "And next to Professor Sugermann sits Mr. Thomas L. Gates, lawyer, civic leader, consultant to the Committee for a number of years."

Now the moderator appeared, and Mrs. Birmingham found herself facing Allen Purcell.

"And I," Mr. Purcell said, "am Allen Purcell, Director of Telemedia." He seated himself at the end of the table, by the water pitcher. "Shall we begin, gentlemen, with a few words about the etymology of active assimilation? Just how did Major Streiter develop the policy that was to prove so effective in his dealings with opposition groups?"

"Well, Mr. Purcell," Professor Sugermann began, coughing importantly and fingering his chin, "the Major had many opportunities to see first-hand the ravages of war on principally agricultural and food-producing areas, such as the livestock regions of the West, the wheat fields of Kansas, the dairy industry of New England. These were all but wiped out, and naturally, as we all know, there was intensive deprivation if not actual starvation. This contributed to a decline of over-all productivity affecting industrial reconstruction. And during this period, of course, communications broke down; areas were cut off; anarchy was common."

"In that connection," Doctor Gleeby put in, "many of the problems of decline of moral standards inherent in the Age of

Waste were vastly intensified by this collapse of what little government there was."

"Yes indeed," Professor Sugermann agreed. "So in following this historic pattern, Major Streiter saw the need of finding new sources of food . . . and the soil, as we know, was excessively impregnated with toxic metals, poisons, ash. Most domestic herds had died off." He gazed upward. "I believe by 1975 there were less than three hundred head of cattle in North America."

"That sounds right," Mr. Purcell said agreeably.

"So," Professor Sugermann continued, "Moral Reclaimers as they operated in the field in the form of teams —" He gestured. "More or less autonomous units; we're familiar with the technique. . . . Encountered a virtually insoluble problem, that of feeding and caring for the numbers of persons coming across from hostile groups operating in the same area. In that connection I might add that Major Streiter seems to have foreseen long in advance the continual decline of animal husbandry that was to occur during the next decade. He took steps to anticipate the decline, and of course historians have made a big point of the aptness of those steps."

Professor Sugermann sighed, contemplated his clasped hands, then went on.

"To fully grasp their situation, we must picture ourselves as living essentially without government, in a world of brute force. What concepts of morality existed were found only within the Reclaimers' units; outside of that it was dog-eat-dog, animal against animal. A kind of jungle struggle for survival, with no holds barred."

The table and five men dissolved; in their place appeared familiar scenes of the first postwar years. Ruins, squalor, barbarians snarling over scraps of meat. Dried pelts hanging from slatternly hovels. Flies. Filth.

"Large numbers of opposition groups," Professor Sugermann continued, "were falling into our hands daily, thus complicating an already catastrophic problem of creating a stable diet in the devastated areas. Morec was on the ascendancy, but nobody was so idealistic as to believe the problem of creating a unified cultural milieu could be solved overnight. And the really sobering factor, evidently recognized early by the Major, was the so-called 'impossible' faction: those groups who could never be won over, and who were doing the most harm. Since Reclaimers were principally operating against those 'impossibles,' it was only natural that in the plan worked out by Major Streiter these 'impossibles' would be the most natural sources for assimilation. Further—"

"I must disagree," Mr. Gates interrupted, "if I may, Professor Sugermann. Isn't it true that active assimilation had already occurred, *prior* to the Morec Plan? The Major was fundamentally an empiricist; he saw assimilation occurring spontaneously and he was quick to take advantage of it."

"I'm afraid that doesn't do justice to the Major's planning ability," Mr. Priar spoke up. "That is, you're making it sound as if active assimilation just—happened. But we know active assimilation was basic, preceding the autofac system which eventually supplanted it."

"I think we have two points of view here," Mr. Purcell, the moderator, said. "But in any case we agree that Major Streiter did utilize active assimilation early in the postwar years to solve the problem of feeding rural populations and of reducing the numbers of hostile and 'impossible' elements."

"Yes," Doctor Gleeby said. "By 1997 at least ten thousand 'impossibles' had been assimilated. And numerous by-products of economic value were being obtained: glue, gelatins, hides, hair."

"Can we fix a date for the first official assimilation?" Mr. Purcell asked.

"Yes," Professor Sugermann said. "It was May of 1987 that

one hundred Russian 'impossibles' were captured, killed, and then processed by Reclaimers operating in the Ukrainian area. I believe Major Streiter himself divided an 'impossible' with his family, on the Fourth of July."

"I suppose boiling was the usual processing method," Mr. Priar commented.

"Boiling, and of course, frying. In this case Mrs. Streiter's recipe was used, calling for broiling."

"So the term 'active assimilation,'" Mr. Purcell said, "can historically be used to encompass any form of killing, cooking, and eating of hostile groups, whether it be by boiling, or frying, or broiling, or baking; in short, any culinary method apropos, with or without the preserving of by-products such as skin, bones, fingernails, for commercial use."

"Exactly," Doctor Gleeby said, nodding. "Although it should be pointed out that the indiscriminate eating of hostile elements without an official —"

Whamp! went the television set, and Mrs. Birmingham sat up with dismay. The image had gone dead; the screen was dark.

The discussion of "active assimilation" had been plunged abruptly off the air.

23

ALLEN SAID: "THEY cut off our power."

"The lines," Gleeby answered, fumbling around in the darkness of the office. All the lights of the Telemedia building had vanished; the TV transmitter above them was silent, and projection had ceased. "There's emergency generating equipment, independent of city power."

"Takes a lot to run a transmitter," Sugermann said, pulling aside the window blinds and peering out at the evening lanes below. "Getabouts everywhere. Cohorts, I think."

Allen and Gleeby made their way down the stairs to the emergency generators, guided by Allen's cigarette lighter. Gates followed; with him was a technician from the transmitter.

"We can have it back on in ten or fifteen minutes," the TV technician said, inspecting the generator capacities. "But it won't hold. The drain's too great for these; it'll be on for a while and then — like now."

"Do the best you can," Allen said. He wondered how much of the projection had been understood. "You think we made our Morec?" he asked Sugermann.

"Our un-Morec," Sugermann said. He smiled crookedly. "They were standing by for the point-of-no-return. So we must have made it clear."

"Here goes," Gates said. The generators were on, and now the overhead lights flickered. "Back in business."

"For a while," Allen said.

The screen of Janet Purcell's television set was small; it was the portable unit that Allen had brought. She lay propped up on the couch in their one-room apartment, waiting for the image to return. Presently it did.

" . . . d," Professor Sugermann was saying. The image faded and darkened, then ebbed into distortion. "But broiling was favored, I believe."

"Not according to my information," Doctor Gleeby corrected.

"Our discussion," the moderator, her husband, said, "really concerns the use of active assimilation in the present-day world. Now it has been suggested that active assimilation as a punitive policy be revived to deal with the current wave of anarchy. Would you care to comment on that, Doctor Gleeby?"

"Certainly." Doctor Gleeby knocked dottle from his pipe into the ash tray in the center of the table. "We must remember that active assimilation was primarily a solution to problems of nutrition, not, as is often supposed, a weapon to convert hostile elements. Naturally I'm gravely concerned with the outbreak of violence and vandalism today, as epitomized by this really dreadful japery of the Park statue, but we can scarcely be said to suffer from the nutritional problem. After all, the autofac system—"

"Historically," Professor Sugermann interrupted, "you may have a point, Doctor. But from the standpoint of efficacy: what would be the effects on these present-day 'impossibles'? Wouldn't the threat of being boiled and eaten act as a deterrent to their hostile impulses? There would be a strong subconscious inhibitory effect, I'm sure."

"To me," Mr. Gates agreed, "it seems that allowing these antisocial individuals merely to run away, hide, take refuge at the

Health Resort, has made it far too easy. We've permitted our dissident elements to do their mischief and then escape scot-free. That's certainly encouraged them to expand their activities. Now, if they knew they'd be eaten —"

"It's well known," Mr. Priar said, "that the severity of punitive action doesn't decrease the frequency of a given crime. They once hanged pickpockets, you realize. It had no effect. That's quite an outmoded theory, Mr. Gates."

"But, to get back to the main discussion," the moderator said, "are we certain that no nutritional effects would accrue from the eating, rather than the expulsion, of our criminals? Professor Sugermann, as an historian, can you tell us what the general public attitude was toward the use, in everyday cookery, of boiled enemy?"

On the TV screen appeared a collection of historical relics: six-foot broiling racks, huge human-sized platters, various cutlery. Jars of spices. Immense-pronged forks. Knives. Recipe books.

"It was clearly an art," Professor Sugermann said. "Properly prepared, boiled enemy was a gourmet's delight. We have the Major's own words on this subject." Professor Sugermann, again visible, unfolded his notes. "Toward the end of his life the Major ate only, or nearly only, boiled enemy. It was a great favorite of his wife's, and, as we've said, her recipes are regarded as among the finest extant. E. B. Erickson once estimated that Major Streiter and his immediate family must have personally assimilated at least six hundred fully-grown 'impossibles.' So there you have the more or less official opinion."

Whamp! the TV screen went, and again the image died. A kaleidoscopic procession of colors, patterns, dots passed rapidly; from the speaker emerged squawks of protest, whines, squeals.

" . . . a tradition in the Streiter family. The Major's grandson is said to have expressed great preference for . . ."

Again silence. Then sputters, garbled visual images.

" . . . so I cannot over-emphasize my support of this program. The effects —" More confusion, sounds and flickers. A sudden roar of static. " . . . would be an object lesson as well as the contemporary restoration of boiled enemy to its proper place on —"

The TV screen gurgled, died, returned briefly to life.

" . . . may be the test one way or another. Were there others?"

Allen's voice was heard: "Several, supposedly now being rounded up."

"But they caught the ringleader! And Mrs. Hoyt herself has expressed —"

More interference. The screen showed a news announcer standing at the table with the four participants. Mr. Allen Purcell, the moderator, was examining a news dispatch.

" . . . assimilation in the actual historic vessels employed by her family. After tasting a carefully-prepared sample of boiled conspirator, Mrs. Ida Pease Hoyt has pronounced the dish 'highly savory,' and 'fit to grace the tables of —'"

Again the image died, and this time for good. Within a few moments a mysterious voice, not part of the discussion, became suddenly audible, declaring:

"Because of technical difficulties it is suggested that viewers turn off their sets for the balance of the evening. There will be no further transmission tonight."

The statement was repeated every few minutes. It had the harsh overtones of the Cohorts of Major Streiter. Janet, propped up on the couch, understood that the powers had regained control. She wondered if her husband was all right.

"Technical difficulties," the official voice said, "Turn off your sets."

She left hers on, and waited.

"That's it," Allen said.

From the darkness Sugermann said: "We got it over, though. They cut us off, but not in time."

Cigarette lighters and matches came on, and the office re-merged. Allen felt buoyed up with triumph. "We might as well go home. We did our job; we put the japery through."

"May be sort of hard to get home," Gates said. "The Cohorts are hanging around out there, waiting for you. The finger's on you, Allen."

Allen thought of Janet alone in the apartment. If they wanted him they'd certainly try there. "I should go after my wife," he said to Sugermann.

"Downstairs," Sugermann said, "is a Getabout you can use. Gates, get down there with him; show him where it is."

"No," Allen said. "I can't walk out on you people." Especially on Harry Priar and Joe Gleeby; they had no Hokkaido to lose themselves in. "I can't leave you to be picked off."

"The biggest favor you can do us," Gleeby said, "is to get out of here. They don't care about us; they know who thought this japery up." He shook his head. "Cannibalism. Gourmet's delight. Mrs. Streiter's own recipes. You better get moving."

Priar added: "That's the price you pay for talent. It shows a mile off."

Getting a firm grip on Allen's shoulder, Sugermann propelled him to the office door. "Show him the Getabout," he ordered Gates. "But keep him down while you're out there; the Cohorts are the wrath of God."

As Allen and Gates descended the long flight of stairs to the ground floor, Gates said: "You happy?"

"Yes, except for Janet." And he would miss the people he had assembled. It had been satisfactory and wonderful to concoct the japery with Gates and Sugermann, Gleeby and Priar.

"Maybe they caught her and boiled her." Gates giggled, and

the match he held swayed. "That isn't probable. Don't worry about it."

He wasn't worried about that, but he wished he had planned for the Committee's prompt reaction. "They weren't exactly asleep," he murmured.

A herd of technicians raced past them, shining flashlights ahead along the stairs. "Get out," they chanted. "Get out, get out." The racket of their descent echoed, and faded.

"All finished," Gates snickered. "Here we go."

They had reached the lobby. T-M employees milled in the darkness; some were stepping through the barricade out into the evening lane. The headlights of Getabouts flashed, and voices called back and forth, a confusion of catcalls and fun. The indistinct activity was party-like; but now it was time to leave.

"Here," Gates said, pushing through a gap in the barricade. Allen followed, and they were on the lane. Behind them the Telemedia building was huge and somber, deprived of its power: extinguished. The parked Getabout was moist with night mist as Gates and Allen climbed into it and slammed the doors.

"I'll drive," Allen said. He snapped on the motor, and the Getabout glided steamily out onto the lane. After a block he switched on the headlights.

As he turned at an intersection another Getabout rolled out after him. Gates saw it and began whooping with glee.

"Here they come — let's go!"

Allen pushed the Getabout to its top speed, perhaps thirty-five miles an hour. Pedestrians ran wildly. In the rear-view mirror he could make out faces within the pursuing Getabout. Ralf Hadler was driving. Beside him was Fred Luddy. And in the back seat was Tony Blake of Blake-Moffet.

Leaning out, Gates shouted back: "Boil, bake, fry! Boil, bake, fry! Try and catch us!"

His face expressionless, Hadler lifted a pistol and fired. The shot whistled past Gates, who ducked instantly in.

"We're going to jump," Allen said. The Getabout was nearing a sharp curve. "Grab hold." He forced the tiller as far as it would go. "We have to stop first."

Gates pulled his knees up and wrapped himself head-down in a fetal posture. As the Getabout completed the curve, Allen slammed down on the brake; the little car screamed and shuddered, bucked from side to side, and then wandered tottering into a rail. Gates half-rolled, half-fell from the swinging and open door, struck the pavement and bounded to his feet. Dizzy, his head ringing, Allen stumbled after him.

The second Getabout hurtled around the curve and without slowing—Hadler was still the bum driver—struck its stalled quarry. Parts of Getabout flew in all directions; the three occupants disappeared in the rubbish. Hadler's gun skidded across the lane and bounced from a lamppost.

"See you," Gates panted to Allen, already loping off. He grinned back over his shoulder. "Boil, bake, fry. They won't get us. Say hello to Janet."

Allen hurried through the semi-gloom of the lane, among the pedestrians who seemed to be everywhere. Behind him Hadler had emerged from the wreckage of the two Getabouts; he picked up his gun, inspected it, lifted it uncertainly in Allen's direction, and then shoved it away inside his coat. Allen continued on, and the figure of Hadler fell away.

When he reached the apartment, he found Janet fully dressed, her face white with animation. The door was locked, and he had to wait while she untangled the chain. "Are you hurt?" she asked, seeing blood on his cheek.

"Jarred a little." He took hold of her arm and led her out into the hall. "They'll be here any minute. Thank God it's night."

"What was that?" Janet asked, as they hurried downstairs. "Major Streiter didn't really *eat* people, did he?"

"Not literally," he said. But in a sense, a very real sense, it was true. Morec had gobbled greedily at the human soul.

"How far are we going?" Janet asked.

"To the field," he grunted, holding on tightly to her. Fortunately it wasn't far. She seemed in good spirits, nervous and excited, and not depressed. Perhaps much of her depression had come from sheer boredom . . . from the ultimate emptiness of a drab world.

Holding hands they trotted onto the field, gasping for breath.

There, outlined with lights, was the great inter-S ship preparing for its flight from the Sol System to the Sirius System. Passengers were clustered at the foot of the lift, saying goodbye.

Running across the gravel field, Allen shouted: "Mavis! Wait for us!"

Among the passengers stood a dour, slumped-over man in a heavy overcoat. Myron Mavis glanced up, peered sourly.

"Stop!" Allen shouted, as Mavis turned away. Clutching his wife's fingers Allen reached the edge of the passenger platform and halted, wheezing. "We're going along."

Mavis scrutinized the two of them with bloodshot eyes. "Are you?"

"You've got room," Allen said. "You own a whole planet. Come on, Myron. We've got to leave."

"Half a planet," Mavis corrected.

"What's it like?" Janet gasped. "Is it nice, there?"

"Cattle, mostly," Mavis said. "Orchards, plenty of cachinery crying to be used. Lots of work. You can tear down mountains and drain swamps. You'll both sweat; you won't be sitting around sun-bathing."

"Fine," Allen said. "Exactly what we want."

In the darkness above them a mechanical voice intoned: "All passengers step onto lift. All visitors leave the field."

"Take this," Mavis instructed, pushing a suitcase into Allen's hands. "You, too." He handed Janet a box tied with twine. "And keep your mouths shut. If anybody asks you anything, let me do the talking."

"Son and daughter," Janet said, pressing against him and holding onto her husband's hand. "You'll take care of us, won't you? We'll be as quiet as mice." Breathless, laughing, she hugged Allen and then Mavis. "Here we go—we're leaving!"

At the edge of the field, at the railing, was a clump of shapes. Clutching Mavis' suitcase, Allen looked back and saw the teenagers, There they were, clustered in the usual small, dark knot. Silent, as always, and following the progress of the ship. Weighing, speculating, imagining where it was going . . . picturing the colony. Was it crops? Was it a planet of oranges? Was it a world of growing plants, hills and pastures and herds of sheep, goats, cattle, pigs? Cattle, in this case. The kids would know. They would be saying it now, speaking it back and forth to one another. Or not speaking it. Not having to, because they had watched so long.

"We can't leave," Allen said.

"What's the matter?" Janet tugged at him urgently. "We have to stay on the lift; it's going up."

"Ye gods!" Mavis groaned. "Changed your mind?"

"We're going back," Allen said. He set down Mavis' suitcase and took the package from Janet's hands. "Later, maybe. When we're finished here. We still have something to do."

"Lunacy," Mavis said. "Lunacy on top of lunacy."

"No," Allen said. "And you know it isn't."

"Please," Janet whispered. "What is it? What's wrong?"

"You can't do anything for those kids," Mavis said to him.

"I can stay with them," Allen said. "And I can make my feelings clear." That much, at least.

"It's your decision." Mavis threw up his arms in disgust and dismissal. "The hell with you. I don't even know what you're talking about." But the expression on his face showed that he did. "I wash my hands of the whole business. Do what you think is best."

"All right," Janet said. "Let's go back. Let's get it over with. As long as we have to."

"You'll keep a place for us?" Allen asked Mavis.

Sighing, Mavis nodded. "Yes, I'll be expecting you."

"It may not be for a while."

Mavis thumped him on the shoulder. "But I'll see both of you." He kissed Janet on the cheek, and then very formally, and with emphasis, he shook hands with both of them. "When the time comes."

"Thanks," Allen said.

Surrounded by his luggage and fellow passengers, Mavis watched them go. "Good luck." His voice followed after them, and then was lost in the murmur of machinery.

With his wife, Allen walked slowly back across the field. He was winded from the running, and Janet's steps dragged. Behind them, with a growing roar, the ship was rising. Ahead of them was Newer York, and, sticking up from the expanse of housing units and office buildings, was the spire. He felt sobered and a little ashamed. But now he was finishing what he had begun that Sunday night, in the darkness of the Park. So it was good. And he could stop feeling ashamed.

"What'll they do to us?" Janet asked after a while.

"We'll survive." In him was an absolute conviction. "Whatever it is. We'll show up on the other side, and that's what matters."

"And then we'll go to Myron's planet?"

"We will," he promised. "Then it'll be all right."

Standing at the edge of the field were the teen-agers, and a varied assortment of people: relatives of passengers, minor field officials, passers-by, an off-duty policeman. Allen and his wife approached them and stopped by the rail.

"I'm Allen Purcell," he said, and he spoke with pride. "I'm the person who japed the statue of Major Streiter. I'd like everybody to know it."

The people gaped, murmured together, and then melted off to safety. The teen-agers remained, aloof and silent. The off-duty policeman blinked and started in the direction of a telephone.

Allen, his arm around his wife, waited composedly for the Getabouts of the Cohorts.